A WHISPER TO THE MOON

A WHISPER TO THE MOON

DENNIS MACARAEG

Copyright © 2019 by Dennis Macaraeg

All rights reserved.

ISBN: 978-0-9987548-4-0

This novel is a work of fiction. Names, characters, organizations, and incidents are either products of the author's imagination or are used fictitiously. Any resemblance to actual events, locales, businesses, places or persons living or dead, is entirely coincidental.

No part of this book may be reproduced in any form or by any electronic or mechanical means, including information storage and retrieval systems, without written permission from the author, except for the use of brief quotations in a book review.

A WHISPER TO THE MOON

1

No college senior should ever be in a position to find out at the last minute that he needs to take another required class in order to graduate on time. Yet, I found myself in that dilemma.

It was the end of January 1990, my last semester at San Diego State University. I stood at the door of room 130 in Hepner Hall as my heart raced in anticipation. Would I get into that history class? About 50 or so students stood outside the classroom. I knew that only 40 students would be allowed. Craning my neck, I hoped to spot the "crash list" circulating amongst the students. Someone must have taken it off the door. As seconds ticked by, the knot in the pit of my stomach tightened exponentially. I planned everything down to the minute detail on paper, but life's practicality is another thing. Before school started, I thought I would be walking in a cap and gown in four months with no problem; yet as I looked around for the list, my graduation date became dimmer by the minute.

"Damn. Where's that paper?" I mumbled.

From the back of the line, I spotted a student in shorts and a black T-shirt with the university's logo holding the coveted sheet. He handed it to me as if the paper was infected. My knees weakened from disappointment when I read that there were already 40 names listed. A wave of frustration came over me as I pictured myself taking a summer class. I wouldn't be able to graduate this semester after all.

Six years ago, I immigrated to America with my family from the Philippines. The first to graduate in our household, worry coiled around my throat, suffocating me. How would I break the bad news to my parents that I wouldn't make it to the May graduation? I had to think of something right away . . . but what? I needed four classes to graduate and the history class was my last requirement that would complete the degree. Without this class, my graduation would be delayed.

With nothing else to do but to accept my chosen fate, I turned to the woman standing next to me with a backpack slung over her shoulder to pass the list. She parted her honey-colored hair away from her face and took the paper from me.

I thought of heading to the library to look for a course catalog. There had to be another class I could take to meet my requirements.

Wanting to leave, I took a step back when I heard her say, "Is there something wrong?"

Her emerald eyes were focused on my dark hazelnut eyes. I stood an inch shy of six feet. The top of her head was at my eye level. For a brief second, I forgot about the class I had missed enrolling in. I noticed her accent with its slightly nasal tone. As a television and film major, I've watched many foreign films. I was confident it was French.

"What else? I'm screwed."

"You're upset with not getting in the class?"

"Yup. The list is already full and it looks like I'm going to be back here in the summer."

"If I were you, I wouldn't worry about it too much," she said.

"Not to worry? I won't graduate if I don't get in this class. I'll be three units short."

I looked at her in disbelief. She had no concept of what I was going through. With a headache looming over me, I turned around wanting to clear my mind so I could figure out what to do next.

I was about to leave when I heard her say, "Wait . . . I think I can help you with this one."

She took out a pencil from her backpack. I looked over her shoulder—she began erasing her name. I wanted to know who she was, so I could thank her, but it was too late. The line where her name was a few seconds ago was now blank. She gave the paper back to me.

"There you go. It's your lucky day. You'll have a nice and worry-free summer."

"Don't you need the class?" I asked, perplexed with what she had just done.

"It's my backup class. I was about to leave myself. Write your name down before someone beats you to the punch."

Elated with the random gift she had given me, my pulse, which had been beating uncontrollably, began to relax. Just a minute ago, I was paralyzed with the thought of the disappointment on my parents' faces when I told them about my situation. She had saved me from summer school and a few extra months in my apartment.

"Thanks."

"Umm, I know how it feels. It's my last semester too."

"You have no idea how much this means to me. Can I ask you another favor?"

She was silent for a moment. From the expression of concern on her face, I could see that she braced for my next request.

"I can't give you my other class. If that's what you're gonna ask. I'll be here next summer if I gave it to you."

"Oh, not that." I laughed at her reaction. "Can I borrow your pencil?"

I placed the paper against the wall and quickly scribbled my name; a smile zipping on my face, happy that I was fourth on the list. Getting in the class would be a slam dunk.

I turned around to return her pencil.

But she was already gone.

2

When the class finally ended, I stood up and followed my fellow students out of the building. I wanted to get out of this joint, join the workforce and start a career for myself, but a part of me didn't want to leave; I wanted to be a student and stay 22 forever.

The thought of being in the "real world," swimming with the sharks and looking for work seemed daunting. Maybe I should search for an entry-level job in broadcast television. Perhaps I should enroll in a master's program right away. With my passion for photography, maybe I should submit my portfolio to a magazine. My editor mentioned that magazines and other publications are always looking for new and creative photographers.

Then the tendrils of melancholy gripped me, knowing that after four more months, I might never see this place ever again.

Behind me, the bells from Hardy Memorial Tower rang out. From the number of chimes, I knew it was 3:00 p.m. The palm trees swayed in the crisp breeze blowing through campus. I walked with slow steps, unlike my fellow students who were in a hurry to get to their classes. I have been a staff photographer for the *Daily Aztec*, the college newspaper, for two years. The project that my editor assigned me to photograph for the next issue circled in my mind. He needed new photos taken around the county for an article he wanted to include about favorite San Diego sites and attractions like the seals at La Jolla Cove, the beaches in Del Mar, and the Spanish architecture of Balboa Park.

The lemon sun floating high in the sky felt hot on my caramel skin. From the central courtyard, I walked through Hepner Hall's massive archway. I marveled at the whitewashed building with the bell tower on top and thought of my orientation day four years ago. I was a nervous kid back then and didn't know what to expect, let alone know if I would graduate.

To my right, I heard my name being called.

"Robert... wait up!"

I turned to my right and saw my best friend Ryan catching up to me. A journalism major and a senior like me, we're both staffers for the *Daily Aztec*.

"Whassup, buddy?" I asked.

"Have you come up with an idea for the project our editor's been bugging us about?"

"I was thinking about scenic places to visit in the county for students to decompress."

"That sounds good." Ryan scratched his head, looking unimpressed with my proposal.

"That's the only thing I can think of for now," I said apologetically.

"Let's see how our editor feels about that," Ryan responded. The expression on his face suggested neither approval nor disapproval of my suggestion.

"What about the relationships between students on campus?"

"Where on earth did you come up with that? The theme is

about San Diego County and its beauty: pictures of the desert, beaches, and historic places. How'd it end up being about dating? That's way out of left field."

I cleared my throat. "It's still about that. When you and Brooke started dating, remember how you'd complain to me about running out of ideas on what to do?"

"Yup, and . . ."

"Why not put a little spice of love into it? The students will be interested in your article, and my pictures will entertain them. See that over there?" I said, pointing to a couple of students walking in the far distance holding hands, oblivious to university life swirling around them. "And over there," I followed up, pointing to a couple sitting on the grass, lost in each other's company.

"So?"

"See all those people falling in love? They can't be meeting at the same spot all the time. Holding hands and staring at each other in a stinky dorm is kinda cool, but that can get old quick, like my former roommate's socks. They eventually need to go somewhere. San Diego is a lover's paradise."

"I can't argue with that. Students will always be infatuated with each other. Find an idyllic location like Ocean Beach or Palomar Observatory to photograph, and I'll see what story I can write."

"What are you doing later?" I asked. "I can show you what I've come up with."

"I'm meeting Brooke at the greens by Scripps Cottage. She's volunteering for the international tea hour for a meet-and-greet with new students. I'm writing an article about it. Take some pictures for me."

"I guess so," I replied, following him. "Any good news from the newspaper in North County? How was your interview?"

"I was hired. I start in July."

"Congrats!"

"What are you planning after graduation?" Ryan asked, as he tried to keep up with my fast strides.

"Maybe take a couple of months off and go on a backpacking trip abroad and visit the places I want to see, like South America."

"Ooh, some kind of foreign affair. Meet someone and fall in love. Find your arms around a passionate Argentinean señorita and you tango off into the night." Ryan said, winking playfully.

"I like the idea already," I replied. "I might even meet a cute Japanese girl with long black hair while I'm in Kyoto, sipping a hot cup of green tea. Who knows? We might end up on a tatami mat and kiss until dawn."

"Yeah, yeah. If you get lucky."

Such a ridiculous thought. Meggy, my girlfriend of three years, broke up with me six months ago and left for New York. She wanted to put some space between us and cool off while she was away. Although Meggy did say that if we were really meant for each other, we'd come together again. I doubt if that would ever happen. The last thing I wanted was to get involved with someone and end up with a lifetime of regret.

STANDING ON THE CONCRETE PATHWAY, BROOKE, RYAN'S girlfriend, held a sign that read: "Free hot tea and meet new friends."

"Nice that you came," Brooke said, tucking her light brown hair behind one ear. She smiled at me and turned her sky-blue eyes to Ryan who stood next to me. He pecked her on the forehead.

"Why not? I'm getting something free for a change," I said.

"If you're feeling generous, you can start your philanthropic career by donating a dollar, so we can buy more tea and cups," Brooke pointed to the basket on the table.

"Why not just steal some from the cafeteria. I'm sure no one would care," I said, setting my backpack next to her.

"Yeah, tomorrow . . . you'd be taking my mug shot, and Tom will be writing the headline 'the paper cup bandit'. That wouldn't be good."

"That's right. Then I'll steal them from the pizza place across the street."

"Robert . . . Please take nice pictures. You wouldn't survive in Alcatraz."

"Why don't I leave you two lovebirds alone while I take some." I reached into my backpack and retrieved my Minolta 35mm SLR.

I approached the deck area and began formulating a plan for which angles would be best to photograph the foreign students. About 60 of them chatted amongst themselves, speaking English with various accents. Raising the camera to my eye, I waited for a good shot. I had just snapped a photo when one of the students looked at me. This reminded me that self-consciousness leads to unnatural expressions from the subject being photographed when the photographer is too close. I walked to the grassy area further away to avoid being detected and focused on the young people who sat under a tree.

I heard Spanish being spoken by one group, Chinese from five women, and what sounded like German from another group. Though I didn't understand a word they said, the sound of a United Nations meeting a stone's throw away was pleasant to hear. Most of them had probably arrived just weeks ago, and today was the first time they had a chance to mingle with fellow students. Being in a country where their customs and traditions suddenly did not apply would take time to get used to. I felt the same when I first arrived in my late teens.

I set the aperture to a wide setting to blur the background and crouched down for a low angle shot of the Spanish-speaking students. I changed location and zoomed in on the German group—capturing their wide grins as they chatted and laughed.

Photography has always been my shelter in times of stress. Whenever things in my life were dreadful, I would pick up my camera and click away as if I wasn't part of the world I was shooting. And when things were going well for me, the camera hanging on my shoulder would be my constant companion.

About 20 minutes later, I finished the 36-shot roll of film. Satisfied that I had taken enough pictures to pick from, I returned to the bench where I left my backpack. As I was putting my camera away, one of the volunteers with a tray of hot tea approached me.

"Would you like a cup?" The voice sounded familiar. It was the same accent I heard yesterday. "It's hot, so be careful."

I turned around. It was her—the adorable girl who offered her spot to me on the crash list. Her honey-colored hair, parted in the middle, cascaded down her shoulders; the tips touching the top of her sleeveless white blouse that exposed her slender arms.

I took the cup from her, fixating my eyes on her a few seconds longer, hoping she'd recognize me. She just stared back. Feeling embarrassed, I quickly looked away. Her pink cheeks blushed in the mid-afternoon sun.

"Thanks for the warning," I said, slowly sipping the black tea with a hint of mint and orange.

"Have you taken enough pictures? I saw you clicking away from over there." She pointed to the grassy area.

"I think so. I already burned through an entire roll of film."

"For your album?"

"No . . . I'm with the school paper. The pictures are for today's event and next week's issue. You might even be in it, so don't forget to pick up a copy."

"Maybe I will," she said, shifting her hands under the tray.

"Thank you for coming to my rescue yesterday," I said, nervously running my fingers through my black hair.

"For what?" she replied.

"For offering me your spot on the crash list. Otherwise, I would have been up the creek."

"Oh. That was you." Her face lit up. "I thought I recognized you from somewhere."

"Yep. The one and only."

"No problem at all. I was worried that I might not get all the classes I needed in order to graduate, so I signed up for an extra class."

"I was going to return your pencil, but you left right away, I didn't have the chance to give it back."

I reached in my backpack and retrieved the item.

"Thank you," she said.

"There you go. I'm not a pencil thief after all."

I wanted to know her name. Something about her made me feel as if I had already known her in the past. Fear drummed in my chest as I gathered strength to introduce myself. I hate this boy-girl thing. There's nothing more intimidating to a man than the moment when he's about to let the woman he's attracted to discover his intentions. Though asking her name could be a benign act, one's actions give it all away. I could never keep a poker face.

I thought of saying something like, "Hi, I'm Robert. What's yours?" Instead, I just looked her and waited for her to introduce herself first. But what were the chances? Perhaps she would say something like "I'm busy trying to solve world peace, and I have no time for this." Then I thought to myself, she could already have a boyfriend, and I would be doing myself a huge favor if I let her walk away now and forget about her. Besides, what was I thinking? A pretty girl like that won't give me the time of day. Guys were probably lined out the door wanting to ask her out. In her world, I was probably nothing.

There's something intimidating about how a man feels when he approaches a woman he's attracted to; maybe it's the uneasiness stemming from the anticipation of being rejected. With my knees weakening under the weight of my nervousness and fear drumming in my chest, I summoned all my courage and took a step forward ignoring the huge knot exponentially forming in the bottom of my stomach. What did I have to lose? If she told me to get lost, that wouldn't be the end of the world. Maybe I should just let my curiosity go and forget about her.

She took a step back and was about to walk away. The perfect timing to know her was slipping through my fingers. If I didn't act immediately, I would lose the opportunity. It was now or never. I cleared my throat to rid myself of my uneasiness.

"By the way, I'm . . ."

Ryan slapped me on the shoulder. "There you are. I thought you left already."

I slowly peeled my eyes away from her, taking my time. Then glared at Ryan.

"What are you doing, man?" I whispered.

We already had an agreement that if one of us was talking to a cute girl, the other one shouldn't ruin the moment. For a brief second, I thought of giving him another mean look for interfering. This was rule #1, and he broke it big time. Ryan acted like the annoying "drunk guy" at the party.

"Did you forget about our . . ." I muttered under my breath.

"That's why I'm here," Ryan replied, looking irritated. "I'm making your life easy. If you just listen, she's one of . . ."

Brooke approached us and said, "Did you introduce them to each other?"

"That's what I'm trying to get at, but he won't listen," Ryan said with a grin.

"Oh." This time, Brooke looked puzzled.

Brooke turned to the woman standing next to me and said, "Catherine, this is Robert, Ryan's best friend."

"Hi." I smiled sheepishly at Catherine.

I finally understood why Ryan acted strangely. The quick introduction relieved me from further anxiety.

"It's nice finally knowing your name." Catherine balanced the tray on her left arm and waved her right hand at me.

"She makes the best tea," I remarked.

"All I had to do was dunk the tea bag in a cup of hot water. I don't think there's any talent needed."

"You could be a chef someday."

"I can only boil eggs and stick frozen entrees in the microwave."

One of the student organizers interrupted us. From what I overheard, Brooke needed to attend to some issue.

"Excuse me," Brooke said, walking away. "Ryan, can you come please?"

Just a brief moment ago, my throat was dry while figuring out on how to get her name. But now that we were properly introduced, I was tongue-tied.

I looked away from her, pretending that I was amused with the chatter from the students around me. Wanting to break the silence and the rising unease of our situation, I asked the first thing that came to mind, "What's your favorite flavor of tea?"

"Earl Grey, but I'm more of a coffee person."

"There's this thing called iced, blended coffee sold in some coffee shops. Have you tried it?"

"You're not making this up, are you? That's a strange concept to me. I only drink hot coffee with cream," Catherine replied.

"It's refreshing on a hot day."

Brooke returned a few minutes later.

She threw a sideways glance at Catherine and said, "I hate to break up our teatime at the park but..."

"Oh, yeah, I almost forgot we're attending a presentation and don't want to be late," Catherine said, walking to the table and setting the tray down.

"You're still coming to our mini get-together on Friday, right?" Brooke asked.

"Oh, sure. Thanks for reminding me," I said, picking up my backpack from the ground.

"In case you have a hot date, you can bring her too. Just be there by eight," Ryan interjected.

"I don't know about that. Me? The unluckiest guy in love?" I replied to Ryan.

"You never know. That someone might be just around the corner," Brooke playfully said, with a quick glance over her shoulder in Catherine's direction.

"I hope if there's one, she'll turn onto the corner where I'm standing."

Brooke hooked her thumb in one of Ryan's belt loops, and he returned her affectionate gesture by placing his arm around her shoulders.

Ryan reiterated, "Don't be late or you might miss the action."

A tinge of jealousy poked me in the ribs. I asked myself if the day would come when I'd be like them—wrapped in a blissful realm of being in love. It reminded me that Meggy liked to tuck her hand in my back pocket while we walked together.

Catherine came back, now wearing her backpack. "It was nice meeting you, Robert."

"You too, Catherine," I said, waving. "Till next time."

With Brooke's cryptic message, I had a hunch that Catherine would be there on Friday as well. It has been awhile since someone intrigued me. I didn't know if it was her charm or the way tiny dimples formed in her cheeks when she smiled at me that stoked my interest in her. It has been too long since I'd been struck by Cupid's arrow.

Forty-eight hours seemed like an eternity.

3

Clusters of red-orange clouds hung in the darkening sky as I drove to downtown San Diego. The cool wind blew my hair as my 1980, green MG convertible sped along the two-lane 163-freeway—cutting through the lush greenery of Balboa Park. At the end of the highway, I turned in the direction of the Gaslamp Quarter. Tourists filled the crowded sidewalks, posing for pictures in front of the Victorian-style buildings. I had come to like this place where the city of modern San Diego was born. I thought of the horse-drawn carriages on the streets more than a century ago as the primary means of transportation. Lovers walked, holding hands as if the night belonged to them. On the corner, a middle-aged musician with a beret on his head serenaded the crowd with sweet sounds from his polished brass trumpet.

I headed down Fifth Avenue passing by endless rows of restaurants. Smells of fried chicken wings, brick oven pizzas, and freshly baked cinnamon rolls wafted in the air. The powerful sound of live rock and roll music floated through the front doors of the clubs. Patrons with smiles on their faces stood in long lines to get into the trendy bars. Laughter from the reveling crowd filled the fresh night air. The gas lamps with their nostalgic, black cast iron posts and ornate glass globes lined the streets. My car inched forward, and I slowly burned time sitting in traffic.

Like an apparition, the gelato shop, where Meggy met with me and broke the news that she was moving to New York appeared to my left. It came without warning and shocked me to the core. Never in my wildest dreams would I expect those words to be uttered by the girl I thought would meet me at the altar one day. Yet, as she looked me straight in the eye, she explained that she needed time to understand her life's direction. I didn't protest, though it was hard for me to accept my chosen fate. Through the large glass window, two teenagers shared an ice cream sundae. I was tempted to walk up to the boy and tell him to enjoy his mocha crunch now because one day, his heart would be crunched up. They seemed full of love and longing for each other. In contrast, six months ago, my life was in a tailspin.

I ENTERED THE BAR AND GRILL WHERE I NEEDED TO MEET RYAN and Brooke. The place had a rustic look with peeling plaster on sections of the wall exposing red bricks. Wide, wood-bladed fans slowly rotated on the ceiling, circulating the booze-filled air.

Immediately, I recognized some of the students from the school paper holding bottles of beer and some of Brooke's friends from the International Students Committee sipping wine coolers.

I spotted Ryan and Brooke standing in the bar area, holding hands.

"Glad you made it, bro," Ryan said.

"You look professional in your blue jeans and a button-down shirt."

Ryan and I high-fived.

Brooke stepped forward and gave me a light hug. "I made him wear pants."

"Now you know who's wearing the pants," Ryan added with a macho voice.

"I can tell," I replied, winking at Brooke.

"Aren't you getting a drink?" Ryan asked.

I turned to the bartender and ordered a bottle of beer.

While waiting for my drink, I saw Catherine walk through the front door with confidence in her step. Her red heels complemented her white blouse and pink skirt. As soon as she saw Ryan and Brooke, she flashed a big smile and rushed to them.

"I made it," Catherine said, leaning forward and giving them kisses; the kind where their cheeks touched and lips made smacking sounds.

I was glad to see her again; my stomach immediately flipped.

"I'm happy you're here," Brooke said.

"It's nice to get out of my cramped dorm," Catherine replied.

A group of four women walked in. They all had short, dark brown hair. I recognized them as the German speaking students during teatime two days ago.

"Excuse us for a sec. Ryan and I need to talk to them. Can you keep her company?" Brooke asked as she pulled Ryan by his arm.

Wanting to make her feel at home, I asked, "Can I get you something?"

"I'm not good with drinks. What are you having?"

"Chocolate flavored beer."

"First time I heard of that."

"I recently discovered it myself but if you don't like beer, I can get you the local favorite. A margarita."

The bartender placed a basket of pretzels and a bowl of peanuts on the counter.

"I'll share my pretzels if you share your peanuts," I teased.

"That seems to be a fair trade," Catherine replied, a warm glow radiating from her eyes.

I pushed the basket to her. She pushed the bowl closer to me.

"Enjoy," I said.

The bartender placed a glass of strawberry-flavored margarita in front of her. She picked it up and sipped it without using a straw.

"My first margarita in California."

"You're already drinking it like a pro."

"Oh, I have to tell Brooke that I need a ride back to my dorm after the party," Catherine said, searching her immediate area.

"You came alone?"

"Yeah. My next-door neighbor in my dorm gave me a ride here but took off with her boyfriend."

"Do you have a boyfriend who'll show up tonight? I don't want to get into a fistfight by talking to you."

"I have none, so you can relax," she replied. A slight smile appeared on her face. "What about you? Do you have a girlfriend that might walk in here any minute? I don't want anyone scratching my eyes out."

"Aah . . . You're safe on that one. I assure you."

I was glad she came alone. I could talk to her freely about anything, but I still beat around the bush so as not to be misconstrued as nosy; it could sour the night.

The noise level swelled in the bar. With her soft-spoken voice, it became difficult to hear what she was saying. I moved closer to her and asked, "Do you want to go to the back? We can do something special."

"Like what? We just met." She said, upping the banter.

"No. Nothing like that," I replied, slightly laughing.

I pointed to the game room in the back.

"The pool table?"

"Yes. Just a friendly game since Ryan and Brooke left us here to fend for ourselves."

I set up the billiard balls in the triangle and centered it on the table, then asked, "Have you played before?"

"No, but you can teach me the basics," Catherine said. Her eagerness to learn was painted across her face.

I handed her a cue stick and the blue chalk. "You must swipe the chalk on the tip of the stick each time you shoot the cue ball, so it doesn't slip."

I started the game with the break shot. The balls scattered all over the table.

"Now, it's your turn."

Catherine bent forward, rested the front of the cue on her left hand. She made the shot, but the tip of the stick missed the cue ball's center point and slipped to the side.

"Darn." She muttered in frustration. "I'm not good at this."

"Your bridge is too far from the cue ball. Move it closer." I pointed to her hand.

"Like this?" She asked, moving her left hand closer to the cue ball but still too far.

Instinctively, I bent forward beside her, placed my hand over her left hand and helped her align her shot. My swollen bicep touched her arm. Her honey-colored hair cascaded in my face and a jasmine-scented perfume drifted to my nose. She turned to me with a slightly embarrassed look on her face. A thin layer of sweat formed on the tip of her nose.

"Aim for the object ball with the cue ball and shoot."

Catherine pulled the stick back and took the shot. The solid green six ball fell in the corner pocket.

"Lucky shot," she said, excitement in her voice.

"You got it. You'll probably beat me on our next game."

IT WAS 2:00 AM, LAST CALL, WHEN THE NIGHT ENDED. THE REST OF the group wanted to go to a late-night diner but because Brooke was tired and wanted to go home, we decided to end the night.

Standing on the curb, Brooke, Catherine and I waited for Ryan to pull up with his car.

"Sorry to have ignored you two all night," Brooke said.

"Robert was great company," Catherine said.

"What did you guys talk about?" Brooke sounded as if she was probing for more.

"About his photography," Catherine said.

"They're working on a column for the school paper. He's taking the photos, and Ryan is writing the article. You didn't tell her about that, Robert?"

"It's not a big deal," I said.

"So, what did you and Ryan come up with?" Brooke asked.

"We'll be concentrating on the touristy places in San Diego: the beaches, the mountains, and the desert. Places that students could go. And since most of them are broke, maybe somewhere free."

"Like a guidebook for students?" Catherine asked.

"On the cheap," I replied.

Ryan pulled up in front of the bar. He got out of the small four-seater and opened the passenger side door. The back was filled with all kinds of boxes. He pushed them to one side but could barely make a space for Catherine to sit. I went to the other side of the car. Through the open window, I held onto the boxes, so they wouldn't fall over her head.

"Are you sure I'll fit inside?" Catherine asked, a look of concern on her face.

She slid into the rear passenger seat. Turning her legs sideways to fit more comfortably, but the boxes were in the way. She reached for the seatbelt buckle, but the locking mechanism was buried in the boxes, and she couldn't fasten it.

The ride back to her dorm wouldn't take long, but it looked like she wouldn't be very comfortable in the tiny space in the back, plus it would be unsafe.

"I could take you home," I said, turning to Catherine. "If that's OK with you?"

By the confused look on her face, she seemed to be contemplating which was the better option—riding with me in comfort or being squeezed in for the 20-minute trip.

"You're a safe driver, right?" Catherine asked. A hint of tease in her voice.

"I promise to deliver you in one piece. And I have a working seatbelt."

A slight smile broke on her face. "Between losing circulation in my legs and a possible blood clot, I think riding with you is a better option." She got out of the car.

"You got her, bro?" Ryan asked.

"Yeah . . . I'll take her back to her dorm."

As Catherine and I waited for Ryan and Brooke to get situated in the car, I could tell that she was just as excited as me to be pushing the boundaries of our curiosity on each other. Meeting someone new is like going to a place I've never been. I can only rely on what the other travelers tell me. The rest, I have to figure out on my own.

The events of the night were happening too fast. A few days ago, I was happy with the possibility of meeting her again. But now, I had Catherine all to myself. Each minute was a step closer to truly getting to know her, a step I didn't know if I was ready for.

Only time would tell . . .

4

Catherine and I stood on the sidewalk and watched Ryan and Brooke's car merge with the rest of the vehicles heading to the freeway. I had never been alone with any woman ever since Meggy left. For the first time in months, Catherine's presence felt as if it was essential oxygen to revive the part of my heart that had been slowly dying.

"Where did you park?" Catherine asked, looking down the road. "I hope it's not in the scary part of town."

"A few blocks that way," I said, pointing to North Harbor Drive's general direction. "It'll probably be a 15-minute walk back to my car. You're with me. No one will bother you."

"And what should I do in case something goes down?"

"When I say run . . . run real fast." I replied with a fake running motion.

"Not with my heels on. I can barely walk straight with these."

"Luckily, I parked in the touristy area."

"I haven't been out of my dorm much since I arrived. Are there sights to see along the way?"

"Not through Broadway. Fifth Avenue ends at the Convention Center. If we walk along the water, we'll reach Seaport Village. It's a bit touristy, but it'll be a nice walk."

STRANGE HOW CHANCE PLAYS SO MUCH IN ONE'S LIFE. A WEEK AGO, if you had asked me if I'd be with a beautiful girl on a Friday night, I would have laughed and said that no such luck ever comes my way. Yet here I was, walking with Catherine. I pretended to look at the restaurants and shops to her right and stole quick glances at the same time. I wondered if the night was some sort of trick and only a one-time deal. Would she quickly disappear just as fast as she appeared in my life? Would she be gone again once the night was over, like a shooting star streaking across the black sky?

A man singing and playing guitar on the street corner caught our attention. Catherine stopped and listened to him.

"'Piña Colada.' One of my favorite songs and drinks," Catherine said.

"You know what that song's about?"

"I never really analyzed it. Something about infidelity?"

"It's about a guy who was bored with his lady and started looking through the personal ads. Turned out his wife or girlfriend placed the ad," I said.

"Would you ever do that?"

"Look through the personals when my lover gets boring?"

"Something like that," she said.

"I really don't know," I replied without taking my eyes from the man singing. "I think a couple goes through phases where they doubt if they're still attracted to one another. The trick is to make every day special by caring."

We continued our stroll through the empty streets. The people partying were mostly gone. Few cars zipped past by us. Eventually, we reached the end of Fifth Avenue.

"And that's the San Diego Convention Center," I said, pointing to the white canvas roof that looked like the sails of a ship; lights burnished through the glass of its massive windows.

"Is Seaport Village there?" Catherine asked.

"Close."

I led her behind the building. We walked along the marina. A fleet of sailboats lined the docks—their masts pointed to the star-filled night and rocked side-to-side as the water below flowed in and out of the bay.

We stopped by the breakwater. Catherine leaned over the white seawall. The reflection from the nearby lights danced off the rippling water on the bay. I stood next to her and listened to the soothing sounds of the water slapping on the rocks.

With a side glance, I studied the curve of her jaw and her smooth cheeks. Her shoulder length hair with curls on the end lifted slightly with the light breeze. When she turned in my direction, her eyes locked on mine for just mere milliseconds but with intensity. For a brief second, I was tempted to ask, "Is it really going to be you?" I could tell she was just as curious about who that fellow was next to her. We quickly looked away, embarrassed, pretending to be entertained by the tourists walking past us.

"There's something I've wanted to ask you. I hear an accent when you talk. Where are you from?" I asked.

"Andorra."

"Does it get to be a pain wearing wooden shoes?"

"You got me confused with the Dutch."

"Oh. I'm sorry. I am pretty sure that's a country somewhere in Europe, but where?"

"It's wedged between France and Spain. And you? Are you Hawaiian? I've always wanted to go there," Catherine asked, looking straight at me.

"No . . . Ever heard of the Philippines?"

"Of course. I know where it is. Just not how to spell it. How many Ls and Ps are there? It's like spelling Mississippi. It's too confusing."

"Even I misspell it sometimes," I said. "I'm assuming you're an exchange student?"

"Good guess. I just came here to finish my degree. Are you also here to study?" she asked.

"No. I live here. I'll be looking for work after graduation and a permanent place to live or in my parents' basement. Whichever comes first," I laughed.

"Why did you move here?"

"Long story. See those gray giants?" I pointed to the naval ships docked across the bay.

"You snuck in on one of those to get here and pretended you're one of the sailors?"

"That would be hard. I don't even know how tie a knot. My uncle joined the U.S. Navy in the '70s and sponsored my family to immigrate here," I replied, taking my eyes away from the ships and turning to her. "Were you born in Andorra?"

"No, France. We moved to Andorra when I was 13. My mom is from northern Italy, and my father is French."

"You're majoring in...?"

"Accounting."

"You like crunching numbers all day?" Surprised to hear her response.

"I just wanted to learn a skill, so I can earn my own money. Do you want me to do your taxes?"

"I don't have a real job yet."

"Is photography your major?"

"It's just a serious hobby for now. It's actually television and film."

"You want to be a movie director or write the script for the next big blockbuster?"

"It depends. Will you star in one of them?"

"Will I get my own dressing room and a personal chef?" Catherine asked playfully.

"That would depend on the budget. If it's a major Hollywood production, then I'll even throw in two assistants. If it's an indie film, we'll have boxed lunches and rented trailers," I replied, winking. "I actually want to work in broadcast television someday. Produce or direct shows."

"Just like those guys whispering in their headsets."

"Could be, someday. You and Brooke have the same major?"

"Yup, we always joked that we'll open up a firm and work together from dawn until dusk until we're old maids."

"Funny you say that. Ryan and I talked about working together in a newsroom, too. Me in the video department and him as a reporter."

Catherine turned around and leaned against the wall. She looked up at the people having dinner at the restaurant on the pier.

"I can't believe we're in our final semester," she said, changing the subject.

"Four months to go and school's done."

"We've been going to school nonstop since we were in kindergarten." Catherine said.

"I've often wondered how my life will be when school is finally over."

"Do you have any difficult classes this semester?" she asked.

"Just the history class that I inherited from you, which I'm not a big fan of. Other than that, I should be able to coast along fine. How many classes do you have?" I asked.

"Three," Catherine replied.

"Are you attending graduation here or . . . ?"

"I'm planning to go to the ceremony back home, but I could technically do it here too. I'll have to see."

Catherine put her arms together. I could tell that her muscles were shivering from the late-night chill. I took off my jacket and offered it to her.

"You won't be cold?" she asked.

"My sweater is warm enough."

"Thank you," she said, slipping her arms through the sleeves.

We followed the narrow brick alleyway until it ended in a courtyard. Above us, the half moon floated in the velvet sky, shrouded with a sheet of transparent clouds diffusing its glow. I took a mental snapshot of the side of her face and recorded her image deep in my memory like a camera would on film. Perhaps, I could retrieve that picture on the days when I wasn't with her.

We continued our stroll and stumbled upon a toy store. The wooden dolls and trucks neatly arranged on the shelves looked out the window for the passersby to see. They reminded me of the projects in my woodworking class.

"When I was in high school back in the Philippines, I made an airplane from wood with the internal frame of the fuselage and wings exposed for a science fair. I didn't know how to start building one, so I went to the library and tried to check out a book with an airplane diagram, but the librarian wouldn't let me take it home."

"You didn't hide it in your jacket and walk off with it. Did you?"

"No. I came back the following day, pulled the book from the shelf and hid in a corner where nobody could see me. I flipped to the page where the diagram was and ran a pen several times along the book fold, then tore off the page. I stuffed it in my pocket and put the book back on the shelf. Then went home and built my airplane."

"Did you win?"

"I got a second-place ribbon. My classmates were impressed, but I felt guilty for what I did. I went back to the library after the awards ceremony and taped the page back in the book to rid myself of guilt."

"The librarian should have let you borrow the book," Catherine added.

"What I did was still wrong. When the school officials returned my airplane, I destroyed it when I got home. I was so bummed by what I had done."

"Robert, we all do things that we're not proud of," Catherine remarked.

"I guess you're right. Sometimes doing what is right, even for all the right reasons, can sometimes be the wrong thing to do."

Though the CLOSED sign was displayed, the front door was wide open. Three employees were inside going through each aisle with clipboards in their hands. It was apparent they were doing inventory. Catherine stepped inside the store; I followed her. She told one of the employees that we're not buying anything and asked if it was all right to look around. We were allowed to check out the items for sale.

"What kinds of things did you play with when you were a little girl?" I asked.

She picked up an oval-shaped figure with a picture of a doll painted on the front and showed it to me. "This."

"A wooden egg?"

"It is called a matryoshka," Catherine said.

"What is it?"

"I think they're also called nesting dolls. The smaller doll fits in the bigger doll. They all fit in the largest one. I played with these when I was a little girl. I arranged them on the windowsill like a small army and talked to them on rainy days when I couldn't get out of the house."

Catherine pulled open the top of the dolls, then put them

back together and arranged them on the shelf from the biggest all the way down to the smallest.

"So that's how you play with them." I said, amazed to see how the dolls were assembled.

"I have a little secret that I've never told anyone."

"You shot them one by one with a BB gun? I won't say a word, promise. Scout's honor," I said, raising three fingers.

"I'm not cruel to my toys. When I was a little girl, my cousin came to our house with her matryoshka set and forgot it after leaving. While playing with the dolls in the garden, I dropped the smallest piece in a bush. I frantically searched but lost it. When she came back a few days later to take her doll set back, I pretended that nothing was out of the ordinary, scared of being so irresponsible and maybe causing a fight between us."

"Do you think she discovered what you did?"

"I think so because she was a bit cold to me the next time we met."

"I guess I'm not the only one who has a skeleton in the closet," I said.

"But the following year, I saw a matryoshka set at the store that looked just like the one I lost, so I gave her the set as a Christmas gift."

"I guess we both eventually atoned for our sins in the end."

Catherine strode down a small aisle with a display of boxed sets of wooden blocks and animal figures.

"What toys did you play with when you were a boy?"

I looked around the store and found some slingshots hanging on the wall.

"This one," I said, picking up one of the slingshots and stretching the elastic rubber.

"How do you shoot?"

"Oh easy, you get a piece of stone or a nut, tuck it in the

leather pocket and pull the elastic band. All you have to do is center your target in the middle of the 'Y' then release."

It was almost four in the morning when we left the downtown area. The traffic on Interstate 5 northbound flowed smoothly with only sparse cars speeding along. As I approached Interstate 8 heading east that would take us straight back to the college area, I noticed the orange traffic cones blocking the entrance and road repair trucks parked on the shoulder. With no other choice, I continued on until reaching the Clairemont area, then headed straight to Interstate 805 south.

We were on the bridge in Mission Valley when we heard loud screams from police sirens and saw strobe lights flashing past us. The cars in front began slowing down and moving to the side; closer to the edge of the bridge. Then, all southbound traffic was at a standstill.

"Looks like there's an accident," I commented.

Catherine rolled her window all the way down and pulled herself out and sat on the door. Her body stuck halfway out.

"Come over here, Robert, see how high we are."

Since there was no movement at all, I pulled the parking brakes to lock the wheels. Wanting to have a clear view of what was going on, I pulled the roof down and blasted the heater for comfort.

The early morning air felt chilly on our cheeks, but we were rewarded by the view of the stars twinkling like sparkling jewels in early morning sky.

"Looks like we are going to be here until the end of the semester," I said.

"I should have refused your ride, bit the bullet and rode with Brooke."

"But you wouldn't have been able to tour downtown."

"Or I might already be in the hospital by now with a blood clot," Catherine said.

"Looks like this bridge might collapse from the weight of all these cars."

"Nothing's going to happen to the bridge," Catherine replied with a nervous laugh.

"It's possible, and what if it does? You could end up spending your last day with me."

"Highly unlikely."

"I think it's confession time just in case something happens."

"You and your apocalyptic prediction. But yeah, just in case, what do you want to know?"

"Am I allowed to ask anything? You must answer truthfully."

She turned to me and cocked her head sideways.

"Depends. I still have secrets that I wouldn't tell you. What if we lived? Then you'll have something to blackmail me with."

"Are you rich? If not, I wouldn't worry too much about it. Unless you've hidden a body in your basement, but I don't think you're that kind," I replied.

"Fire away."

"What if next Saturday is your last day here on Earth? What would you do?"

"Watch the clock until everything goes black."

"Not an answer."

"Contact everyone close to me. Past and present. Apologize to the people I hurt. Tell everyone that I love them before drifting to the other side," Catherine said. "And you?"

"Do something I haven't done before. I can do a lot crazy stuff in a week."

"Like what? Skydiving?"

"No . . . not that crazy."

"Something like watch the sunrise with someone I just met."

She was silent for a moment as if debating what to tell me.

"And if that someone you just met agrees, where would you take her?"

Thinking of the best places to experience daybreak, I replied, "I think I have an idea since it's almost six in the morning. Are you hungry? I think you might like this."

"Now that you mentioned it, my last meal was over eight hours ago."

I stopped by the bagel place I frequented in the college area. I picked up two cups of coffee with cream and two freshly-toasted everything bagels with bacon, pepper jack cheese and eggs. When I returned to the car, I handed the bag to her.

"Where are you taking me?" Catherine asked.

"You'll see. You may add this experience to your Bucket List," I replied, releasing the clutch and stepping on the gas pedal.

LOCATED A FEW MILES FROM THE UNIVERSITY, MT. HELIX overlooked the city of La Mesa and the eastern parts of San Diego.

It was still dark outside. Carefully, we walked up the steps, with the bag of bagels and coffee in our hands, until reaching the middle of the amphitheater.

Catherine sat next to me. I took one of the wrapped bagels from the bag and handed it to her.

"The coffee is decaf, so you'll be able to sleep later," I said.

"I can't believe I've been up for almost 24 hours."

"Can't remember the last time I stayed up all night," I said.

The morning air was cold, but the hot coffee was comforting. We faced east and waited for the dawn to arrive.

Catherine took a bite of her sandwich and asked, "Do you like living in America?"

"Of course. It's my home now. I came here with my family when I was 16," I said. "Why do you ask?"

"Nothing. It's just . . . I'm so far from home. I don't know anybody here."

"There's Brooke, Ryan and . . . well, me."

An airplane landing at Lindbergh Field screamed in the distance. Catherine turned toward it and commented.

"I came through that airport."

"Is it your first time here?" I asked.

"No. I went to Florida four years ago just after high school with my family. We met Brooke and her folks."

"I wore a suit on my flight coming here. I couldn't move freely in my tight airline seat."

"On my connecting flight here, about a quarter of the plane was filled with salespeople. They were all wearing suits and looked uncomfortable."

"You know something cool happened during the flight. I asked the pilot if I could check out the cockpit. I was making model airplanes only several months before, and there I was in the cockpit of a 747 at 35,000 feet."

"Were you scared when you first arrived?"

"No, not really. I was just clueless about how I would live my life in my new home. I'd only known America by watching television shows like *Sesame Street* and movies like *JAWS*. I had no idea if Americans my age would accept me or if I'd even find a girl to like."

"Is there someone special in your life?" Catherine asked.

"Before, but not anymore."

"How come?"

"It's hard to explain. She left me for an apple."

"An apple? She's not Eve, is she?"

"The Big Apple—New York. She decided to move there, away from me."

"That's sad."

"And you? Anyone in your life?"

She took a deep breath, shifted her eyes to a spot in the far distance.

"No. Not anymore. He's the reason why I came here. We're unofficially done with each other."

"You're either together or not."

"He cheated on me, but I have no proof. The thing was, my feelings for him changed because he wouldn't be straight with me. I didn't want him anymore."

"It must have been hard to duck the subject when you were together?"

"I kinda avoided him. Weeks went by, then our situation got worse."

"Must have been hard for you."

"When I told Brooke about my situation, she invited me to come here while I tried to figure things out. It all worked out because the university I attended back home agreed to accept the classes I'd be taking here so I'll be graduating on time too. I left Andorra without saying goodbye to him."

A tiny sliver of orange light appeared somewhere from the eastern side. As minutes passed, the mountains in El Cajon slowly began to appear as if they were watercolor paintings. The silhouettes of trees in front of us formed dark outlines. Bit by bit, the city of La Mesa slowly woke up. The straight two-lane roads and houses built on the hills emerged in the dawn light.

"I hope you're not getting bored," I said.

"With this spectacular view? And you, entertaining me with all your stories?"

"Just making sure."

"I've never had an outdoor breakfast at dawn. This is perfect."

The white cross appeared behind us, looking over our shoulders as if trying to protect us.

We ate our breakfast in silence while we waited for the sun

to come up. We ran out of things to say to each other. Like clockwork, the dark sky turned into a haze of light blue. The twinkling stars were swallowed by the scattering light from the ascending eastern sun.

I was beginning to feel tired but being with Catherine kept me going. It had been such an intense day. It was a day like I've never experienced before, and Catherine was a woman like no other. I was seeing my old self again. A torrent of amorous feelings came over me with no inhibitions. But beneath it all, a cloud of doubt hung over me. I wondered if pursuing what I felt about her would be the right thing to do and if my heart was ready to open up again.

I turned to Catherine as the golden rays of the early morning sun lit the side of her face. It was the best ten hours I've ever spent with anyone.

THE MORNING SKY WAS BRIGHT WHEN WE ARRIVED AT HER DORM. It was almost 7:00 a.m. The speckles of stars had disappeared, and the transparent moon was fading in the sky.

"Thanks for the ride. You're only five hours late." Her voice sounded playful.

"If I knew that I was being timed, I would have driven my Ferrari. But the deal was to get you home in one piece, right?"

She stayed in her seat for a few moments longer as if she didn't want to leave. The glow from the halogen lights in the parking lot illuminated the contours of her face. Through the corner of my eye, I admired her lips—red like berries. Probably so sweet to taste.

"Don't be a stranger when I see you back on campus," she said.

I could tell from her demeanor, she seemed interested in seeing me again. I thought of asking for her phone number and calling her later in the week, so we could do something together. With her ex-boyfriend still in the picture and the fact that she'd be going back to her family after graduation, I remained quiet. Things might not work out between us.

My logical brain told me: It would be better to smile and walk away while my heart was still intact. When I wake up, the magical night will be nothing but a dream, and I'll forget that it ever happened.

But my heart dictated another idea: Why not take a chance? It's time to love again. She could be the right one for me. The heck with the consequences. If she likes me too, then things could work out between us. Tomorrow will take care of itself.

"Here's your jacket back." She began pulling her arm out of the sleeves.

"You don't have to take it off. I don't want you to catch a cold. Just return it when we see each other again."

"Are you sure?"

Catherine hooked her finger on the handle and pushed the door open.

"No problem at all. Later, alligator." I made a salute gesture.

"Thanks for being my tour guide. You know where I live now. I'm on the top floor, so drop in anytime," she said. "In a while, crocodile."

I parted with this lovely woman knowing last night wouldn't be the last time we'd see each other.

5

The bright sun floated high over the Pacific Ocean when I arrived at Torrey Pines State Reserve on Saturday. Zach, Pedro, and Jake—part of the group of at-risk students that I volunteered to teach photography to—were already waiting for me in the parking lot. They had cameras in their hands with eagerness painted on their faces, ready to take some pictures.

Two years ago, Meggy had asked me if I'd be interested in taking portraits of some high school students who couldn't afford to pay a professional photographer to shoot their photos on location the day of their prom. She had already been a volunteer taking them out on hiking trips and general social events. When a few of them expressed an interest in photography, I decided to volunteer my time.

"Are you guys ready to hike and for some cool photo lessons?"

We hiked up the mountain, staying on the trail. The Santa Ana wind coming from the desert felt dry as it shook the branches and the leaves of the rare Torrey Pines.

I stopped by the trees and set up the tripod.

"Sometimes, by setting the shutter speed on slow, we can get nice effects. Set it to about half a second, then a second, and let's see what happens. The leaves and the nearby bushes fluttering in the wind should blur a bit and create a painted effect."

I stood to the side while they mounted their cameras on the tripod and took turns taking photos.

When the three finished taking pictures, we continued with our hike and followed a trail zigzagging on the side of a cliff. We walked past hikers taking their time. Wanting to pace our hike, I told the boys to take a rest at the overlook and enjoy the view of the grey-blue sea that looked like a convex of floating glass.

Spotting green tubular plants with tiny purple and yellow flowers with broad petals near the trail, I said, "These are good subjects when taken with a wide aperture. The background is a blur while the subject is sharp. Don't forget to apply the Rule of Thirds. Put the subject slightly off-center for a more dramatic effect."

Zach, Pedro, and Jake crouched down and busied themselves with their compositions.

My time with Catherine the other day swirled on my mind. It was something else. Unscripted, with the series of events unfolding with pure impulse. I wondered if the sour taste of loneliness lingering in the back of my throat was the reason I yearned for her. Maybe meeting her could wash away the bitter aftertaste of my break up with Meggy. I wasn't even ready to start seeing other women yet. I just wanted to graduate from college and concentrate on getting a career, hopefully in broadcasting, so I could plot the next step in my life. I needed a bearing so I could navigate my next move. The woman I loved before had burned me and jumping into someone's arms wasn't something I had planned.

We hiked down to the beach. The dried pine needles and

twigs on the soft soil crackled beneath my feet. While searching for another subject to shoot, I came across the spot where Meggy and I sat together for hours. She painted the tiny sunflowers and wind poppies growing on the side of the hill while I listened to my headphones. Six months had gone by so fast. Back then, we were together almost every day, holding hands as if never wanting to let go of each other. I was lost in the moment of our crazy love affair, yet I never thought those heavenly days we were living in would come to a screeching halt.

I popped open a new can of film and inhaled its fresh out-of-the-box smell, then handed it to Zach to load into the camera. It never ceased to amaze me that a roll of film, never seeing the light of day, once exposed, would eventually store memorable images that would last for years.

I wondered what Catherine was doing at this very moment. Was she thinking of me too? Maybe I should go to her dorm and invite her to hang out with me. She did say I could drop by anytime.

Aren't things simple anymore?

When a person likes someone, doesn't he just follow his feelings and tell the other person what he honestly feels? Being with her felt so easy, but I knew we were on borrowed time. Even if we ended up seeing each other, Catherine would eventually return to her country. We would probably write to each other often. Later on, it would decrease to an occasional birthday card —a Christmas card, perhaps. Weeks would turn into months until our correspondence became a chore. Both of us would desperately try to hang on to the feeling we once had. Eventually, while on the phone, I would sense her disinterest as she speaks to me in a monotone voice. She might tell me that she got back together with her old boyfriend. In her letter, I would read something like, "Maybe it would be better if we ended the affair." Our fun time together was just part of the foreign experience. She would eventually forget about America and forget about me.

Yet . . . why not take a risk on love again, even if it only lasted a semester?

6

I got on one knee and began shooting rapid fire as the demonstrators holding signs about "Acid Rain" flooded the quadrangle near the Aztec Center. I was on assignment covering the latest happening on campus. Initially, I focused on a poster with pictures of factories emitting grey smoke into the atmosphere and mixing with the clouds. When it rains, the polluted droplets contaminate forests and lakes.

The demonstrators began walking in the direction of the administration building. I followed them hoping to get a dramatic shot for the paper.

Near the campus bookstore, I shot the last frame. With the crowd thinning and already with plenty of footage, I wound the roll of film and placed it in the canister to have it developed later. As I was putting my camera away, I saw a sign that said, "Bargain Wednesdays." Finished with my class for the day, I decided to stop by and check it out. At the table marked "Half Off," books, T-shirts, and team pennants were neatly arranged. While scanning the items, I found a black and white coffee table book of Yosemite with photos by Ansel Adams for five dollars. I flipped through the pages, hoping to learn some techniques from the master photographer.

Just as I turned around to pay, to my delight, I saw Catherine standing by the rack of T-shirts several feet away, waving at me; her lips spread into a gleeful smile.

"You never came back for your jacket," she said, walking toward me.

"Oh, hi. I forgot all about it. I wanted to call you, but I don't have your number. I didn't want to barge into your dorm without calling first."

"You could have asked Brooke, and you're welcome anytime."

As I looked at her, I wanted to pull Catherine into my arms and lock her in a tight embrace and tell her that I wanted her. Something seemed different about her. Perhaps seeing her in full daylight. I remember seeing the monuments in Washington D.C. at night. Though the statues moved me, they looked more impressive in the bright sunlight when I came back the following day. The first time I saw Catherine, she was in a hurry. The last time I was with her was at night. There was something different today. Maybe it was the bright afternoon light highlighting the smooth skin of her face.

"I didn't think of that. Did you find something interesting?" I asked.

"I'm thinking of getting this for a dollar, but I don't know if I'll use it," she said, holding a stationery set.

"You can buy me a jacket with the school logo, and you can keep my jacket hanging in your closet," I said.

"I don't know if I would look good in your Indiana Jones jacket," she replied, laughing.

We paid for our items and walked outside the store. Standing by the entrance, we ran out of things to say to each other but at the same time didn't want to part ways. I wanted to stretch out our conversation. Maybe I should comment on the weather. Perhaps the current price of gas. Pulling my backpack strap tighter on my shoulder, I cleared my throat, then said, "If you're not busy, would you like to have pizza with me?"

She said nothing. Her eyes darted to the students entering the front door. As I waited for her response, a thousand things crisscrossed in my mind. I thought our personalities fit well when were together a few nights ago. It was a lot to assume from our encounter. But as I sensed hesitation in her reaction, I wished I had just said my goodbyes and walked away.

"That would be nice, but I can't."

She had been giving me signals that she was interested in me too. Her response confused me. The stab of rejection pierced my chest. Damn. Bad timing. Stupid me. I should have just played it smooth and acted cool. Droplets of sweat were emerging on my temples, getting heavier by the second and ready to trickle down my cheeks. Now she knew that I had turned our encounter up a notch. She seemed receptive when she commented earlier on why I had not picked up my jacket. This vibe I detected was probably wrong.

"No problem," I replied, trying to act as if being turned down was nothing at all.

"I'm going to the museum with the girl who lives next door for my art appreciation class and eating with her afterward," she said. Her eyes were apologetic.

Her face curled into a look of pity. Perhaps she didn't want to lead me on and hurt my feelings. What could I say? Catherine would eventually return to her country when the semester ended. Getting involved was probably not a good thing for both of us. The air around me was suddenly stifling. I glanced at the students standing near us. I wondered if they heard her reject my invitation. My skin felt hot and for a second, all I wanted was to run away and never to be seen again.

Wanting to save face from being shot down, I said, "No big deal. I'll see you at one of Ryan and Brooke's impromptu get-togethers next time."

I took a step back. I was about to walk away when I heard her say, "If you want, you can pick up your jacket now. We're not leaving for about a half hour."

"I . . . don't want you to be late for your museum trip," I said.

"No . . . Not at all. I'm the one who should be thankful for you giving me a ride last Friday. I didn't mean to sound like I wanted to get rid of you."

"Are you sure? I don't want you to feel like you have to fit me into your busy schedule."

"Busy schedule? I'm a college student. I have nothing but time. I'll even make you tea and share a panettone as thanks for lending me your jacket and the mini-tour of downtown you gave me."

It was strange how the series of events quickly changed. The air blows east. The wind blows west. A second ago, I was down. Then I was up. First, she told me she couldn't have lunch with me. Now, she was inviting me to her dorm.

My heart began doing cartwheels inside my chest.

7

As we entered the front door, excitement tickled me in anticipation of seeing Catherine's room.

We approached the resident clerk, a thin Asian girl with a serious expression on her face.

"My friend Robert. We're going to my room to work on some papers," Catherine lied.

Her eyes stared at us, looking unconvinced with Catherine's explanation, but she waved us through anyway.

As we walked down the narrow hallway, I tried to dodge the residents running in and out of rooms. A boy in shorts clutching a pile of dirty laundry ran past me. I peeked inside one of the open rooms. Three students were inside playing a board game. The bed was unmade. An electric fan sat on top of the microwave oven. Clothes hung on a rack, exposed. Privacy seemed not to exist.

"What paper are we working on?" I asked, laughing.

"I had to say that. She asks too many questions."

Catherine unlocked her door, and I followed her inside. Her room was small. The bed was neatly made, and her books were arranged in order of their heights on the bookshelf. I rested my backpack against the wall and walked toward the window.

"You have a terrific view from up here," I said. "Where's your bunkmate?"

"She moved several rooms down with her best friend."

"Nice. You're here by yourself."

"The pigeons in the parking lot keep me company."

She pulled open a drawer, retrieved an electric kettle, then stepped inside the bathroom and turned on the faucet.

"Do you like dorm living?" I asked.

She plugged in the kettle, then replied, "It's OK. Some of the students who live down the hall get noisy, but I can tolerate them. I put on my headphones at night until I fall asleep. Do you also live in a dorm?"

"I live in a one-bedroom apartment a couple of miles from here."

A few minutes later, the kettle whistled. Catherine poured boiling water into two mugs with tea bags. She handed me my drink. I sat on the chair next to the window while she sat on the edge of her bed holding the hot cup.

"Can I ask you something personal, Robert?"

"No. I'm not a serial killer. Just in case you're wondering."

"I don't think serial killers would be concerned about not graduating on time."

"I guess you're safe with me. Sure."

"You and your girlfriend were together for so long. Why did you decide to end it? Did your passion for each other just fizzle?"

I took a deep breath, then answered. "We couldn't agree on the same flavor of gelato."

"Over an ice cream flavor?" Catherine asked, perplexed.

"Just joking. She broke up with me in a gelato shop in the Gaslamp Quarter. We passed it on our walk."

"That's sad. I guess you hate the flavor you picked that day?"

"My favorite is chocolate. I won't let anyone ruin my love for it. Actually, our breakup wasn't mutual. She decided it was over. She wanted to do something different and discover things for herself."

"Really?"

"She didn't want me to be part of her life anymore. Before she left for New York, she told me that it would be best if we were free from each other. She wanted to experience new things. That if we were meant to be together in the future, our paths would cross again. I doubt it, though."

Catherine placed the mug on the floor, lay on her side, and put her hand under her cheek. "It's strange that you two separated because she desired freedom. My ex-boyfriend, well, he yearned for a different kind of freedom for himself."

Wanting to lighten the mood, I said, "Here's what I'm thinking."

"What?"

"A wacky sitcom based on what happened to us."

"Ahh . . . my side of the story wouldn't be that exciting," Catherine said.

"Has he contacted you?"

"About a week before I came here. He was buying me nice things and wanted me back, but when I asked him about his infidelity, all he did was dodge the question. I think I was just trying to keep us together. He longed for the same life our parents had."

"It happens."

She sat up and said, "I wrote to him a few days after I arrived here. I told him not to expect me after graduation."

"Does that mean you are really finished with him?" I asked, sounding hopeful.

"Looks like it."

"Are you sure about your decision?"

She paused. "Our parents introduced us. They seemed to be more excited for us to be a couple than we were. Our dads are good friends since college; they thought we would make a good couple. That's how everything started."

"How do you feel now?" I asked.

"Relieved, but a bit guilty. Feelings change for no reason sometimes," she admitted.

I put the tea on the desk and looked Catherine straight in the eye. "I thought we were going to get married after college. Have a house, a dog, and 2.5 kids, and it's going to be us forever, and our happy days would never end. Looking back, I didn't even notice the subtle changes, like not wanting to spend time with me when I called her for a quick trip to the mall, or a Friday night movie and popcorn."

"Is that what a 'quickie' means?"

"Ha, ha," I replied, laughing. "That's a little more exciting than shopping or a movie."

"You didn't notice anything different?"

"She was losing interest in me, but I was clueless. By the time I realized what was going on, she already wanted out."

"What will you do if she suddenly shows up on your doorstep and wants you back?"

I shifted my weight in the chair then replied, "Honestly, after everything I went through after she left me, I wouldn't take her back."

"You sure?"

"It's been more than six months now, and I'm not into the on-again, off-again kinda deal," I said.

"That easy?"

"She'll always be a part of my past, but I had moved on and accepted our fate. Things wouldn't be the same between us even if we decided to reconcile."

"And if she tells you that she made a big mistake with tears in her eyes and begs you?"

"Are you sure your major is in accounting and not in film? You sound like a movie director?"

"No, seriously?"

"I will look her straight in the eye before closing the door and say something like 'I don't give a' . . ."

"That's not too original."

"I would simply tell her that I already found someone new," I replied with conviction in my voice.

"Have you?" She asked with a flirty smile.

I felt the hairs stand up on the back of my neck with her daring question. Pushing the boundaries of our banter, I replied, "I feel I'm off to a good start and working on it as we speak."

Looking surprised, her eyes grew slightly bigger. Her cheeks turned red. She quickly took her eyes off me and looked out the window.

Suddenly, I felt the room temperature rise several degrees. My response might have been too daring, too close to the edge of the cliff and could have scared her away. I waited a few seconds for a response, but she was quiet. Wanting to cool things off, I commented, "We've been sitting here for more than half an hour. Are you sure your classmate didn't forget about you?"

"What time is it?" Catherine asked.

She sprang off the bed and headed out the door. I followed her, wondering what she had in mind. She knocked on the door next to her room. Seconds later, a girl with long black hair answered.

"My gosh," the girl said with what I could decipher was a Portuguese accent. "I forgot about our trip to the museum. My boyfriend is here. Can we do it some other time?"

"That's OK," Catherine said. Disappointment in her voice.

"Which museum were you planning to go to?"

"The art museum in La Jolla. The tickets I got are only good for today."

"That's too bad," I replied.

"Maybe next time," she said, walking back to her dorm.

"I wouldn't want to see your tickets go to waste."

"There's always next time."

Wanting to do something to make the melancholy on her face disappear, I suggested, "I can take you there if that's OK with you? I have nothing to do for the rest of the afternoon."

Catherine's face lit up. "Are you sure?"

"Very sure."

"I can always go to the library and look through the large coffee table books."

"But those are copies. Why not see the real thing?"

"I don't want to burden you with my schoolwork."

"After helping me out with the class and saving me from a summer session. It's the least I can do. I'll even take you to a late lunch-early supper. My treat. I hope I bribed you enough."

Catherine placed her hand on the doorknob, turned to me and said, "Fair enough. It's mac and cheese at the cafeteria tonight. I want to skip that for a change."

8

Next thing I knew, we were speeding west on the freeway heading to La Jolla. With the MG's black vinyl roof down, Catherine's hair fluttered in the wind. The warm California sun shone on our faces. As I turned to look at her, Catherine turned to my direction at the same time. She flashed a smile at me. I could tell that she was enjoying the ride.

"I've always dreamt of riding in a convertible in California," she shouted over the wind noise. "Just like in the movies I saw growing up."

I didn't know what to say, so I just winked.

It felt good sitting so close to her. Her declaration at the dorm about being done with her boyfriend echoed in my mind. That was good news. I wondered if seeing her again at the international tea hour a week ago and being Brooke's best friend were purely coincidental or prearranged by some gods in the universe playing Cupid.

If our initial meeting was like listening to an old jazz record beginning with a series of random chord progressions that made no sense at all, the missed signals and the misinterpreted words were like misarranged notes on the sheet music. Although it's not easy on the ears at first, the more I listened, the sequence of tones started to make sense. It became clearer. The music got better with each play. I found harmony in her presence. She was like a song stuck in my mind.

It was close to four in the afternoon when we arrived at the museum. The place was virtually empty except for an older couple sitting on a bench looking at the works of art. We approached an oversized painting. Catherine studied the complex shapes of the abstract figures. The artist made angry brushstrokes using thick paints in ultramarine blues and deep purples, as if to shock the observer.

"Sometimes it's hard to figure out what the painters are trying to say," I remarked.

"They paint for themselves and expect the rest of us to understand what's on their mind."

"Looks like the artist threw a bucket of paint on the canvas next to a helicopter lifting off."

"More like behind a jet plane taking off," Catherine added.

"Luckily, we're in a quiet place," I added.

"I miss the silence. I remember when I was a teenager, my cousin and I explored a long, dark tunnel near where we lived. We kept walking until the light at the end of the tunnel became the size of my fist. It was quiet and dark inside."

"You two weren't scared?" I asked.

"Not really. Kids . . . you know . . . not thinking much of dangers. We could hear our breath. We would lean on the curved walls and stay there a few minutes. It was so peaceful inside."

"It's nice to have a special place like that."

"Do you have one?"

"In the darkroom," I said.

"How so?"

"While I'm printing my pictures, I have to wait for the timer to go off with just the red safety light. The room is filled with pure stillness."

Catherine sat at the end of the bench. She crossed her legs and interlaced her fingers on her knee. I sat next to her and propped my chin with my hand as I studied the painting in front of me. We remained quiet as we gazed at the smorgasbord of artwork around us.

After spending about an hour at the museum, I said, "Let's go down to the beach. I want to show you something."

Outside, the sun inched down slowly behind the ocean, casting a soft golden light on the million-dollar homes perched on the side of Mt. Soledad. The palm trees on the street swayed in the fresh sea breeze, their fan-like leaves ruffling effortlessly. We crossed Coast Boulevard and walked beside the cliffs.

Looking out at the vast sea, the waves broke against the sand below. Up high, groups of pelicans settled on top of tall rock formations, waiting for fish to eat just below the surface.

"Where are we going?" Catherine asked. "To one of your secret caves?"

"It's down there in the rocks," I said as we walked past the protected area called the Children's Pool, adjacent to the hook-shaped, concrete breakwater, where the sand-covered seals frolicked in the cove.

I PLANTED MY RIGHT FOOT ON AN ALGAE-COVERED ROCK, CAREFUL not to slip. I faced Catherine and extended my hand. She reached for me; her hand was soft. She tightened her grip. I didn't let go until she was safely down where I stood.

"See those," I said, looking down on the crevices filled with seawater and tiny sea creatures trapped inside.

"How did those animals get there? Crawl in?" Catherine asked.

"During high tide, they drifted in with the water."

"Are they trapped?"

"For now, but when the high tide comes back, they'll float back out to the ocean."

"I've never seen those," she commented.

"They're called tide pools. They're up and down the California coast."

"Thanks for the lesson, Professor Robert," Catherine said, wanting to be playful.

"I volunteer my time as a mentor with at-risk kids. I take them here sometimes. Come on, I'll show you something even better."

I knelt by the edge of the rock and pointed to the exposed tiny shells, shrimp, and sea creatures in the crater. Catherine knelt beside me and looked at the shallow water trapped in the rock. The smell of drying seaweed and saltwater floated in the air. With her forefinger, Catherine touched the tiny sea slug inside.

"They depend on the high tide rushing back for nutrients. Hold out your hand."

I picked up a light-blue starfish sunbathing on a rock and placed it in her palm.

"Here, feel this," I said.

"Does it bite?"

"Only if it's starving," I replied, winking at her.

"It's stiff. I think it's crawling," Catherine said.

"Now lay it back down."

Catherine gently placed the starfish on the rock.

I pointed out the sea anemone, tiny barnacles, and hermit crabs. We looked though several more tide pools and spent the next half hour inspecting each water-filled crevice with different life forms.

"I'm getting hungry. What do you want to eat? My offer is still good," I asked.

"Is there any authentic California cuisine?"

"Burgers, fries, and pizza? I don't know if there is such thing," I answered.

"I want to taste something local."

I thought of introducing her to Filipino dishes like pansit noodles. She might like it, but the place I knew of was downtown, and it would take at least half an hour to get there. Korean food maybe? Cooking her own food on the grill in the middle of the table would be a new eating experience for her, but the restaurant I frequented was several miles down the road.

"I think I know a place that you'll like. Are you feeling adventurous?"

"I'm game."

"It might be something you never had..."

Catherine and I cut across the park, then headed straight down Prospect Street—passing by the bars, restaurants, and galleries with expensive artwork hanging on the walls.

After walking several blocks, we arrived at the Mexican taco shop I frequently visit after surfing. The locals in shorts and T-shirts filled half of the restaurant and stood in line as they waited to order their food. I glanced at Catherine. She looked confused as she studied the menu board. I could tell that she had no idea what to order.

"The seafood in the tacos wasn't picked from the tide pools, right?"

"Relax, you'll see. It actually tastes good. I'll also order other things."

I neatly arranged the different variety of foods in front of her.

"Your fish taco is deep-fried, battered whitefish in a flour tortilla with sour cream. Squeeze a wedge of lime over it and you're good to go."

She studied the toppings of shredded cabbage, chopped tomatoes, cilantro, onion, and avocado.

"Looks good," she said. "I just couldn't picture it in my mind."

"Think of it as fish and chips without the fries."

"How do I eat it?"

"Like this," I said, taking one of the tacos.

After pouring salsa over it, I placed it in my mouth and tilted my head to the side.

Catherine did what I had just demonstrated, lifted the taco to her mouth and took a bite.

"Umm . . . it's pretty good."

"You'll like the next one I ordered," I said.

A few minutes later, one of the workers arrived at our table with the seafood cocktail in a margarita glass.

"What's in it besides the shrimp, chopped tomatoes, red onion, cucumbers?"

"Avocado and octopus."

"Octopus? I don't know if can handle that."

"You gotta be adventurous sometime and eat something new."

"I'll be a couple sizes bigger if you keep feeding me like this."

"Talking about being adventurous, do you want to see the stars over the ocean? It looks like it's going to be a clear night," I asked.

"With all these lights around us?"

"I'll take you to my secret place. Over there," I said, pointing to the mountain on my right.

"Is it to your million-dollar mansion?"

"No. Just a million-dollar view."

At more than 800 feet high, Mt. Soledad towered over La Jolla. I parked the car facing the ocean and collapsed the roof for a 360-degree view of San Diego County. The taillights from the vehicles passing through Interstate 5 created a red line curving between the mountains. The palm trees lining the beach formed dark patterns against the red-orange sky. Scripps Pier stretched out from the beach like a finger reaching the horizon.

When nighttime finally arrived, stars strung like pearls came out.

"Let's name the constellations," I said.

"I hope I get this right. I see the Big Dipper," Catherine said, tracing an imaginary line in the sky above with her finger. "If you connect the dots, it looks like a kite with a tail."

"You're good at this."

She turned to me and said, "Now it's your turn."

I concentrated on the star formations. I looked directly above me, wishing I had paid more attention to my instructor in my past astronomy class instead of daydreaming. I could use that knowledge now. After tracing out the shape of a cluster of stars, I replied, making a "V" shape with my fingers. "That one, I know that. Andromeda, right there."

"Really? How did you see that?" Catherine asked, the tone of her voice unconvinced.

"I just know."

"Isn't Andromeda seen only during autumn in the northern hemisphere?" Catherine laughed at my silly guess. "I think we're approaching spring."

"I didn't know that. OK, I was faking it. It's the only constellation I know because of the story behind it." I turned to her, embarrassed.

"What's it about?"

"Changing the course of a woman's destiny."

"And?"

"Andromeda was going to be sacrificed to a sea monster named Cetus. She was chained to a rock. Just when she was about to be taken by Cetus, her savior, Perseus, changed the monster into stone and saved Andromeda. Something like that."

Catherine looked out at the vast ocean. The tone of her voice turned serious. "Spending a lot of alone time in my dorm every night, I kept thinking if breaking up with Pierre was the right move."

"Self-doubt is a natural feeling."

"One thing I'm sure of, I don't want him in my life anymore."

"How can you be sure of that?"

"We were introduced by our parents at my father's company picnic when we were in our teens. My mother liked him a lot. She told me we looked good together. At first, I was just curious about him, but as time went on, it seemed that our worlds were becoming smaller. We saw each other a lot. We eventually went out on a date, then started hanging out."

"When did you start liking him?"

"Everyone around us assumed we were together. Just like a tiny snowball rolling down a mountain, it avalanched into a full relationship. I eventually liked him and accepted things as they were. I never thought of ending it because our parents had a good time together. I wanted to be like my mom. She is so happy with my dad. I just went with the flow."

"It seems like you just accepted things as they were."

"Things were easier that way. A nice guy and a nice family. What else can a girl want in life? I was like Andromeda in your story, I guess. I put myself in a situation where I was pinned on the rocks for years. My circumstances became like a monster that was about to take over my life. I wanted Pierre, not because of love anymore, but because I wanted to have a life like my parents."

"And how did your fairy tale romance fall apart?"

"I heard a rumor that he was seeing someone in his school. Even if I couldn't prove it, a switch inside of me was suddenly flicked off, shutting down my warm feelings for him. I confided my situation to Brooke; that's when she suggested I come here to cool off and finish my studies. I didn't realize it then, but that decision became my Perseus that broke me free from all the things stifling me."

How does a man know when the woman in front of him is "the one"?

How is a man drawn to the woman sitting across the table? Is it the way she laughs? Or is it the way she lightly brushes the hair out of her eyes? Or is it as primitive as the physical attraction?

I could only be sure of what I felt right at this moment and tell her that my heart was shouting her name. It was the only way to go. Was making a bold move and professing to her what I honestly felt the right thing to do? Just to mention that I wanted her more than as a friend could ruin things, but going on as casual friends didn't feel right either.

The question didn't even have to be asked. I felt it, and damn the consequences if the day came when she would be going back to Andorra. All I had was the here and now, and I wanted her to know about my strong feelings for her.

The parking lot near her dorm was half full when we arrived. I shut the engine and faced her.

"Thanks for the wonderful day," she softly said in my ear. "I didn't expect that a boring trip to the museum would have the added bonus of an adventure."

As I rolled up the window, I said, "Thank you for making my afternoon memorable."

Feeling like an elementary student and not a college senior, I wondered if taking her time to get out of the car meant she was waiting for a goodbye kiss. But where should I kiss her? On the lips would seem too direct and might turn her off. On her cheek might be too friendly of a gesture that could make her think that I only wanted casual friendship. If I plant one on her forehead, she might think it's a farewell kiss from her grandpa.

"I'll walk you to your room."

"It's OK. It's getting late."

"I want to see that you get home safe."

I got out of the car and opened the door for her. Catherine pushed the door open. Extending my hand, she took it and I gently pulled her up.

When we reached the front entrance, we stood outside for a short while. Catherine twirled a piece of hair dangling from her ear with her fingers. It seemed as if she was trying to stretch the night. She looked up at the eastern sky and commented, "Nice moon."

From the tone in her voice, I could tell she was trying to fill the silence in the empty courtyard.

"I heard that if you whisper to the moon a message that you want to tell someone that you're too shy to tell in person, the moon will relay it back in the other person's ear while they sleep," I said.

She stepped closer to me and wrapped her arms around my waist. I didn't expect the gentleness of her embrace. I pulled her tight against my body and held her in a long embrace. I knew that our connection unlocked our mutual feeling of attraction for each other. A lump formed in my throat. I wanted to say how I felt about her, but my mouth felt dry. When I sensed her arms relax, I slowly separated from her. Still inches away from each other, I studied the sharp curve of her jaw and her smooth cheeks for a few seconds longer. The moment was right, and my heart urged me to follow my desire.

"Why are you staring at me like that?" she asked, looking straight into my eyes.

I slowly reached for her hand and curled my fingers around hers, noticing her clear nail polish. She didn't pull away. Euphoria skyrocketed me into the stratosphere as my heart banged against my chest wall. She squeezed my hand with a firm grip. We held hands tightly as if one of us was falling off a cliff and the other was holding on for dear life. She had already taken residence in me, and the timing couldn't have been more perfect to tell her what I was feeling.

"I'd been attracted to you ever since you offered me a cup of tea, and I think about you day and night."

She looked away from me and concentrated her gaze at a point somewhere in the corner of the square as if searching for an answer on what to tell me. A few seconds later, she looked back at me and said, "I don't know, Robert. You have stoked my curiosity too. Do you think that following what we feel for each other is the right thing to do? Our walk in downtown last week and today have been some of the most exciting days in my life."

"It has been for me too. That's why I'm telling you how I feel."

Stroking my cheek with her thumb, she said, "Is this how you want us to keep going?"

"Yes. I want you to be mine. This intense feeling I have for you, I've never felt this way with anyone."

"I don't know if doing what feels right would be best for us. You've been hurt in the past, and I'm running away from someone."

"Being with you fulfills me."

"We both know how painful a love affair can be."

Her response surprised me. I thought she enjoyed being with me.

The cool air suddenly became too thick to breathe. Moments ago, she embraced me with fervor, yet now her downcast eyes avoided my gaze. She loosened her grip. I slowly let go.

I didn't know what to say next, and all I could do was to stand in front of her in silence wondering what was going through her mind. As seconds ticked by, a piece of eternity chipped away from my soul.

She unzipped her handbag and pulled out the key to her room. As the double doors opened, she said, "Thanks for the wonderful evening. I really enjoyed it."

As blood oozed out of my fractured heart, her final goodbye was the coup de grace I never want to hear.

How did it turn out this way? I thought things were going so well between us. I stood frozen not knowing what to do. I thought of calling out her name like in the movies before I lost her in my line of sight and telling her that my intentions were pure. Instead, I watched helplessly as she disappeared in the hallway, leaving the shattered pieces of my heart scattered on the ground.

9

I cringed at the idea of going back to school. Just a week earlier, I was filled with happiness knowing I would see Catherine somewhere on campus where we would share a snack, and I'd tell a joke or two. Opening up and telling her how I genuinely felt was a big mistake. If I had just maintained our friendship as it was, I would still be seeing her. But not telling her I wanted more than a casual friendship while continuing to hang out as friends didn't feel right either. I took a risk, and it backfired. I stalled, spun, crashed and burned. Now, I might never see her ever again.

Days turned into weeks. I tried to forget about Catherine and concentrate on my routine. I thought about the way she reacted when I professed my feelings for her. Her eyes darted away from me as if I was a total stranger. I was surprised with the immediate distance she put between us. Maybe it wasn't really her fault. Perhaps, I misread the non-verbal messages that made me think she liked me too. Our situation was like a jigsaw puzzle scattered on the floor. Putting the pieces of what-ifs together seemed hopeless. I understood that we both had issues in our past, but that shouldn't dictate what we felt for each other now.

OF THE FOUR CLASSES THAT I HAD TO FINISH BEFORE GRADUATION —English, history, philosophy, and biology—the history class gave me the biggest headache. Sitting at my desk, I could see my professor at the blackboard writing the midterm's test results. With the class size of 40, there were 10 As, 5 Bs, 15 Cs, 6 Ds and 4 Fs. Lines of worry formed on my forehead. With the stack of test papers in his hand, he went to each desk distributing them. My professor placed the test paper in front of me. Immediately, I saw the big letter "D" with a circle marked in red and screaming at me. My heart dropped from disappointment and my arms went limp. I blamed myself for being irresponsible and distracted. I really needed to focus more on my schoolwork and pass this class.

With every ounce of energy I had left in me, I attended my classes and sat in the back of the classroom like a zombie. I ignored the invitations to the latest parties my schoolmates asked me to attend. Meeting someone new wasn't on the top of my list. Slowly, the icy coldness of loneliness began to eat me up. I asked myself why I was even trying to learn all this senseless data from my biology class, dates in history that no one really cared about, and in my English class, why my professor gets so upset about a misplaced comma that most readers would probably ignore anyway.

ARRIVING AT MY APARTMENT COMPLEX, I NOTICED A BAND OF cumulus clouds had gathered in the far distance. It looked like there might be rain. I opened the front door. My cold and lonely apartment hit me in the face. Setting my backpack on the counter, the little red blinking light on the answering machine caught my attention. I pressed Play, imagining that Catherine had left me a message saying something like, "I'm in my room alone and just want you to come over and make passionate love to me." Instead, Ryan's voice squawked through the one-inch speaker.

"Buddy, long time no see. Please call me."

I punched his number on the keypad. On the second ring, Brooke picked up.

"Hi, Brooke."

"Glad you called. Have you seen Catherine lately?" Brooke asked.

I could sense concern with her inquiry. Pausing for a moment, I thought of telling her what had happened between Catherine and me. Maybe she could be the go-between and fix the mess I created. I could ask her to reach out to Catherine and hopefully, arrange for a meeting. But with Catherine's last words, her message spoke loud and clear. She didn't want to get involved, period, and I should stay away. The whole situation could get worse if I didn't give her space to think things through herself.

"No," I said, trying to sound casual.

"Strange. I haven't heard from her, either. Oh well, here's Ryan."

"Are you OK, man? You sound a bit down."

"I'm good," I lied.

"You got some pictures for me? I need to start writing the article. It's due next week."

"Oh yeah, I almost forgot about that. I'll print some tonight."

"Just do them tomorrow. Wanna join us later? We'll be hanging out at the Irish pub around nine. The one near the Mexican taco place."

I thought of jumping back in my car, so I could forget about Catherine for a few hours. At least I could come home tired and go straight to bed. After contemplating what to do, I decided to stay home.

"I got a few things to do. Enjoy your night with Brooke."

I stepped out on my balcony and slumped in the chair, took a big gulp from my iced tea and stared at the gray-black sky. By now, the clouds overhead had covered the stars. The past week played in front of me. Catherine's words echoed in my mind: "We both know how painful a love affair can be." She was right. We had no business falling in love, especially with each other. Our worlds were so far apart, at least with distance. What was wrong with me? Meggy took off with only a vague, "I need to find myself" explanation. I wondered how far I was from the heavenly bliss of finding someone to love and be loved. What mountains do I have to move . . . and how many oceans do I have to cross to get there? It was so very clear; the big hole in my heart could never be filled without Catherine.

Well, Robert (I told myself), forget about the fancy French words she whispered in your ear. Forget about the way her soft hand touched the underside of your elbow. Forget about the way she looked at you as if you were the most important person in the world. Forget about the way she cocked her head when she said goodbye to you.

But how can I forget her when I see her face everywhere in all my waking moments?

I popped in a CD. Duke Ellington's *Take the A Train* began streaming out of the speakers. I wished I could hop on any train to carry me to another dimension, away from the burning feeling in my chest. I closed my eyes and hoped to erase her from my mind. I wished that meeting Catherine was just some sort of twisted thought that I had only imagined in my half-asleep brain. She would be forgotten along with the rest of my dreams as soon as I woke up in the morning.

I went to my makeshift darkroom in the bathroom. I picked

up the enlarger from the floor and placed it on the sink near the wall. I set up the trays with the necessary chemicals to print the pictures. While washing my hands, I caught my image in the mirror. Parting my coal black hair to the side, my bloodshot eyes stared back at me. I flicked the light switch off and drew the black curtain to keep the stray lights from seeping through the gaps around the door with only the red safety light to guide my way around the darkroom. After focusing the image, I placed the strips of negatives on the 8X10 photo paper in the easel to make a contact sheet. I set the timer and made a quick exposure. Ever so carefully, I picked up the photo paper from the edges and dropped it in the tray filled with solution. I flicked the light switch on and looked through the series of images, seeing Catherine in one of the frames, holding the tray of paper cups as she served her fellow students at the international tea hour. I was glad I had randomly taken her picture. Quickly, I made a 4X6 copy.

Done with printing the pictures I needed to show Ryan, I walked to the bedroom, lay on my side, placed Catherine's photo on the nightstand and propped it up against the lamp. Her lips were parted just enough to reveal a tender smile and the smooth skin on her cheeks. Tired and sad, I turned off the bedroom light. The crescent moon floating above the apartment complex's rooftops filtered through the window blinds, forming slices of yellow light on the floor, the nightstand and illuminating part of her picture. I turned onto my other side and pulled the blanket up to my chin. Just before falling asleep, I wondered when I would see her again.

OCEAN BEACH WAS A FAVORITE HANGOUT FOR SURFERS AND SOME guys whom one might argue were throwbacks from the '60s. While walking along Newport Avenue, I strolled past a youth hostel. Young people in their early twenties, from other countries hung around the front steps with sodas and San Diego guidebooks in their hands. I heard Spanish, Italian, and some strange-sounding European language I couldn't place being spoken. The first time I heard these many languages being spoken, Catherine was on the periphery. Now, she was miles away.

I stumbled into a shop selling hippie items. The smell of strawberry-scented incense filled the store. Leather wallets, belts, and different types of chains were hanging on the racks. I looked up to see giant posters of Led Zeppelin, Bob Marley, and other great musicians from the '70s on the walls.

Closer to the beach, I walked past a music store selling old records dating back to the '50s. A country song about a breakup was blasting through the front door. For a second, I was tempted to go inside the store, reach for the record and spin it backwards. Maybe by doing that, I'd get Catherine back. I checked my watch. It was 2:00 p.m. It was almost time to meet Zach, Pedro, and Jake and the rest of their classmates for "Clean the Beach Day."

The kids with their parents and large plastic bags in their hands were already at the beach by the lifeguard station when I arrived.

I walked past Mrs. Redding, the event organizer, with a clipboard in her hand, checking attendance and headed straight to where the volunteers were assembled.

"Hi, guys," I said, waving at them.

"We're ready to go," Jake said.

We walked along the beach looking for discarded items. The volunteers had smiles on their faces as they made a difference on a crisp Sunday morning.

The refreshing ocean wind cooled my head as I placed cans and bottles in my plastic bag. From a distance, I could see the long concrete pier and the fishing poles jutting out from the railings. Out on the water, the local surfers sliced through the waves and balanced themselves on their boards with ease. As I picked up candy wrappers, banana peels, and cigarette butts scattered in the sand, I thought of my situation at school. I really needed to get serious with my studies. My purpose in school was to learn and not get distracted by extracurricular activities that had nothing to do with academics. Graduation was in three months, and I couldn't afford to stay another semester in school.

I must cut my losses with Catherine and move on.

10

I was sitting at my desk in the office of the *Daily Aztec* sorting through a stack of photos I took earlier in the week when Alejandro, my editor, approached me.

"Got some good news for you, Robert," he said.

"Am I gonna get rich, Al?"

"Not exactly, but you can win some money."

"What do I have to do? Join a circus?"

"I got a letter from a local charity. They're inviting local student artists, painters, sculptors, and photographers to submit their work for an auction. The organization you volunteer for as a mentor will be a recipient of part of the proceeds. The top three sellers will win $300 each. I submitted your name. I need about 10 pictures from you. We'll take care of enlarging and framing them," he said, walking away.

The idea thrilled me. I could have extra cash after graduation but more importantly, the new project would keep my mind occupied.

"What's that about?" Ryan said as he approached me.

"He entered my name in some contest."

"I heard about it. He talked to me about attending the event and writing an article. Ready to go?" Ryan asked.

I got up from the desk, hooked my backpack on my shoulder and followed him out the door.

"So, what are your plans later on?" I asked.

"I need to meet with Brooke. We have a situation." The expression on Ryan's face looked serious.

I stopped walking, faced him and asked, "You know, you can always talk to me about whatever's bothering you."

Without beating around the bush, Ryan said, "Brooke is pregnant."

I wanted to congratulate him right away, but I knew better. He had plans that didn't include a baby.

"How long have you known?"

"A week or so. Her period was a month late. She got worried and did one of those urine test things. It came out positive."

"What are you planning to do?"

"This is happening too fast. I really don't know," Ryan said, his voice cracking from worry.

"I thought you were using condoms?"

"I was."

"Did you buy the right size?" I asked.

"I don't remember. Isn't it one size fits all? It might have broken. Dude, I don't know."

We were silent for a while thinking through the situation.

After a minute or so, I said, "I'm confident you'll do the right thing, Ryan."

"I'll love her with or without a baby."

"Where is she right now?"

"At Student Health Services for an appointment. I'm on my way to meet her."

"I'll walk you."

"That's alright. This is between us. I'll keep you updated."

I thought of Ryan's situation. If it happened to Meggy and me, would I have had the courage to drop out from school and ask her to marry me? There were plenty of times when we had unprotected sex, which was a reckless thing to do.

"I'll chill at the garden by the cafeteria and do some reading, then I'll head home. Call me if you need anything."

STILL SHELL-SHOCKED BY THE TURN OF EVENTS, I WALKED TO A vending machine and bought a bottle of peach-flavored iced tea. It seemed like it was just yesterday when we were two 18-year-olds at college orientation four years ago. Now, Ryan was going to be a father.

On my way to the small garden, I walked past art students drawing chalk art replicas of the Mona Lisa and Starry Night on the concrete pavement in front of the administration building.

It was quiet in the flower-scented garden and empty of the usual students chatting amongst themselves. I searched for a shaded area and immediately found a bench near the clumps of lavender and rosemary bushes. An orange flower with its petals turned up to the sky collected sunlight while a yellow butterfly carefully extracted nectar as if making love to a woman.

I reached into my backpack and took out my history textbook and a highlighter. I began marking the important dates that might be on the test. After 20 minutes, my mind started to wander. Ryan and Brooke's pregnancy kept me from concentrating on my studies, so I put the book away. Closing my weary eyes, I saw the bright red dome behind my eyelids, thinking of the 10 best pictures I had taken of San Diego County: Coronado Bridge, its boomerang shape curving around the bay; Balboa Park, its turn-of-the-century buildings; the beaches with sand so smooth to walk on; Cabrillo National Monument with the Old Point Loma Light House standing tall near the cliffs.

From my far right, I heard someone calling my name. It was a familiar voice; one I had come to love over the past month. When I opened my eyes, I recognized Catherine standing a few feet from me. Why was she here? I thought she didn't want to see me anymore.

"Hi," she said.

"You just found me here?" I asked.

"I was with Ryan and Brooke earlier at the clinic. I asked about you. He told me you'd be here. Can I sit next to you?"

"Sure." I slid to the end of the bench.

"So, how you've been doing?" she asked.

"Working on several term papers as usual and the photo assignments from the paper."

"I've been busy too," she said. A tone of reconciliation.

Feeling the urge to explain, I continued, "A few weeks back, when I told you what was on my mind, I just wanted to let you know how I felt. If you feel uncomfortable being alone with me, that's OK. I understand. I wouldn't want that situation to ruin our friendship. Next time we see each other, we can just hang out with a group, so it wouldn't be awkward. Or if you want, just in case we run into each other in a hallway, I'll stay to my right, wink at you and keep going. If that's easier for you."

"No, I'm glad you opened up to me. I like honesty. I've been spending most of the week by myself thinking about all kinds of things. When I left you outside my dorm that night, I wasn't able to sleep. I tossed and turned, wondering if I did the right thing. I worried about you, wondering how you were coping with my rejection."

I picked up the bottle of iced tea and took a quick sip. A tiny stream spilled from the corner of my mouth, then trickled down the side of my neck.

"Your T-shirt is wet," she observed.

"I should have brought a bib."

Catherine pulled out a napkin from her backpack and dabbed the side of my face and chin. She moved closer; her breast pressed on the side of my ribs. Heat formed at the base of my skull followed by nerves radiating down my neck, all the way to the tips of my fingers. Her action confused me. First, she ran away, now we're so close to each other that we could hear each other's breath. I didn't know what to do next. She gazed at me as if I was the only person in the world. With her presence, she was conveying a clear message that she came to see me to declare what was on her mind. With each minute ticking by, I patiently waited for her words. All I could do was to gaze into her eyes full of longing.

The surroundings grew perfectly still. Nothing in the world seemed as important as being with her. I had waited so long to be intimate with her. The motion of the trees swaying and wind sweeping across the pavement ceased. Her face was only inches from mine. Being this close, she was more beautiful than ever. The reality of my hopes and fears converged into the moment. I knew she wanted me too or she wouldn't risk being alone with me. The flowers around us were suddenly saturated with vivid colors. The sky, an endless blue. The leaves, an evergreen of freshness. I couldn't hear anything but the sound of my heartbeat. She began to stroke the side of my neck with her soft fingers.

"You're the one I've been thinking of in my solitude. I wanted to know if I would be able to spend a day without you," Catherine said.

As she revealed her feelings about me, my heart filled with joy. She gently put her hand on my cheek. I reached for it and put it to my lips.

There is a point in an airplane's journey when the pilot must decide whether he should continue the flight or turn around before reaching the halfway point. To turn around for safety was one thing, but to go on crossing the unknown was the only way to get to the desired destination.

The universe whispered in my ear to keep going and risk it all. The timing felt right—the moment perfect. All we needed to do was to seal our mutual understanding with a kiss. Like a damsel on the pier looking out for her lover who had been away sailing across four oceans, she waited for my next move.

I leaned in without taking my eyes off hers. She placed her hand behind my neck and drew me to her. Our lips touched—consummating our mutual attraction for each other. They tasted lovely. Sweeter than all the ice cream in the world combined. I felt her tongue sweep gently in my mouth, connecting our souls. I was the butterfly, and she was the flower. I was on top of the world.

Time stood still.

11

Some unexplainable magic came over me as soon as I knew that Catherine cared for me too. Couples holding hands on campus now seemed to belong to the same fraternity as me. The long line at the library checkout counter and looking for a place to park that seemed to take an eternity didn't feel irritating at all. I walked slower, less hurried to go to my classes. And those birds perched on the light post—the ones I cursed for crapping on the hood of my MG the day after I washed it—their irksome chirps now sounded like love songs. My days had meaning and joy.

With spring break looming on the horizon, a relaxed atmosphere floated on campus. I approached Catherine sitting on a patch of grass beneath a palm tree, reading a novel and sat next to her. She hooked her arms around me and pulled me closer to her.

"I missed you," Catherine remarked, kissing the side of my neck.

I turned and kissed her on the forehead.

"We've only been apart for one day."

"It's long enough for me."

"This school business is keeping us apart. We should leave school and just be together all day, all night," I said.

"And when we run out of food and rent money, what are we going to do then?"

"Live under a bridge?"

"I'm gonna get cold. Plus, I need my espresso maker."

"OK then . . . I guess we have no choice but to finish school and get real jobs."

"Sounds like a better plan."

"Been waiting long?" I asked.

"No. I just got here," she replied. "I have a few more pages to read."

I lay on the green grass and rested my head on her lap. It felt like a soft pillow made of a thousand feathers. As she read, I remained quiet and listened to the sounds of leaves tumbling over the concrete walkway. I filled my lungs with the spring air and thought how lucky it is to be alive and to have her in my life. I wished moments like this would never end.

After ten minutes or so, Catherine closed the book.

"What are you reading?"

"*Les Miserables*. I read it in high school. I'm rereading it for fun this time."

"What's it about?" I asked.

"It's about war and a love triangle. What better story right?"

"I could already tell it's going to be a sad story—one lover is going to be heartbroken."

Catherine placed her palm on my cheek, rubbed it gently and said, "My favorite book ever."

"Can't you just tell me what happens? It's a long book."

"Reading is fun. You get to imagine the scenes in your head."

"I'm a film major. I'm very visual. I'll just have to wait for the movie."

"You don't have to wait for it to come out, the Broadway

musical is coming to the Civic Center in June. You can find out what happens if you see it," Catherine said.

"I need a date. Do you know anyone who'd want to go with me?" I said playfully.

"I might know someone."

"Is she cute?"

"I think so."

"Like you?"

"My mirror image."

"Um, I changed my mind, I'll just ask you. Are you available?"

"Maybe . . . I'll check my planner," she said, pinching my cheek, then kissing me on the forehead.

"So . . . is that a yes?"

"Well, I'll kill you if you go with someone else."

"I guess that would be a yes, then. It's a date."

"Has Ryan talked to you about Brooke?" Catherine asked, tucking the book into her bag.

"About her—uh . . . them, getting pregnant? Yes. I told him not to be rash with whatever they decide."

"Brooke just told me about it yesterday."

"Do you think she's worried?" I asked.

"She's a bit quiet about it. Things are happening so fast. I can't imagine they'll be having a baby by next year."

I couldn't believe that this crazy series of events was going at breakneck speed: Graduation. Looking for work. Babies. A career. Being responsible. And all the benefits and headaches that came with adulthood.

"With that thought," I said, "My editor wants me to take pictures. Then I need to go to a local high school around three. I'm teaching a photography course to some of the students who are going to Italy this summer. Just half an hour or so. Why don't you come with me? We'll have pizza afterwards."

"Where?"

"At the Old Point Loma Lighthouse, then to Mission Beach."

"Is that where the roller coaster is?'

"Why? Wanna ride?"

"I was going to live there with a family friend in Mission Beach. I got a call from my mom the other day. She forwarded my letters to her."

"How come you're not staying with her?"

"Last minute changes. I wanted to be within walking distance from the campus."

Catherine searched through her backpack and pulled out a black, faded address book. She flipped through it until she found the woman's name.

"There's the address."

"We can go after my quick lesson."

UNDER BLUE SKIES SPECKLED WITH COTTON-LIKE CLOUDS, Catherine and I hiked up to the old lighthouse nestled at the tip of Point Loma while a slight sea breeze stroked our faces. To my left, the sight of the perfectly arranged buildings along the shore of downtown San Diego looked like giant upright rectangles.

We entered the lighthouse. The wooden circular staircase creaked beneath our feet as we walked up to the top floors. It felt like we were inside the labyrinth of a nautilus. The corkscrew stairs mirrored my life's strange twist of events. I lost Meggy, then Catherine entered my life.

We peeked in the small bedroom with a low ceiling and basic furniture inside.

"They must have been so lonely here," she commented.

"Just the lighthouse keeper and his wife, together 24 hours a day."

"They must have sat together in that spot for countless hours."

"Isn't it strange? In the end, it's just the two of them who can only rely on each other to survive each day?"

We climbed the stairs until reaching the top floor of the lighthouse. We wanted to go where the massive prism was housed that gives light to the passing ships but couldn't due to metal railings blocking the square opening. All we could do was look up from the bottom.

We sat on the floor and moved closer to the window. Wanting to take a picture of what's down below, I aimed my camera in the general direction of the water. Catherine leaned closer to me and put her arm around my waist and planted a kiss on my cheek.

"This is a first. Getting kissed while composing a shot."

"I'm not distracting you, am I?"

"Nope. These are just pictures," I replied, placing the camera on the floor. "I thought I lost you forever when you told me that getting involved with me wasn't a good idea."

"I was just confused."

"I'm glad you decided to be with me," I said.

"It was a no-brainer."

"What was going through your mind when we were alone in the garden?"

"Something like, 'When is this guy going to make a move?'" Catherine said. Her hand up in the air, pretending she had given up.

"I'm slow in that department."

"Now that's something we can agree on."

"Ha, Ha," I laughed sarcastically.

THERE WERE TEN HIGH SCHOOL SENIORS WAITING FOR ME WHEN WE

arrived at the classroom. The teacher, who was going to be one of their chaperones, introduced me to the group. The students sat in their desks, holding their personal SLR cameras with an eagerness to learn written on their faces. As I set up my camera gear on the table next to me, Catherine headed to one of the desks in the back to watch my demonstration.

"We are all familiar with the focus rings, right? Now point the camera to me. I'll model for you and you focus on my face."

I stood still while they manipulated the focus ring.

"Notice that the background is blurred. Now, focus on the blackboard behind me. Now I become out of focus."

For the next 20 minutes, I taught them about how shutter speed works.

"For moving subjects, you must use a high shutter speed to avoid motion blur, but in order to compensate for that, you need a wider aperture setting."

About five minutes before the presentation was over, one of the students, a girl with auburn hair and wearing shorts and a T-shirt, raised her hand. "Have you been to Italy?"

"No. But I know someone who has been there many times."

"Catherine, can you please come up here?"

Standing in front of the class, Catherine said, "If you are flying to Rome, the airport is far from the city. You would probably want to visit the Colosseum and the best time to go is in the morning to avoid the crowds and the heat. In the early afternoon, you can go to the Villa Borghese gardens. Rent a bike or go for a quick stroll. Then you can go inside the gallery to see Bernini's sculpture of Apollo and Daphne. And late in the afternoon to the Spanish Steps, then to the Trevi Fountain at night."

"Aren't Apollo and Daphne two lovers like Romeo and Juliet?" questioned another girl from the back of the room.

"Not really," Catherine answered. "According to the legend, Apollo offended Cupid. Because of that, Cupid shot Apollo with an arrow that made him fall in love with Daphne. But the arrow intended for Daphne had a reverse effect. She detested him and ran away. When Apollo caught up to her, Daphne asked her father, Peneus, the river god, for help. As she got close to the riverbank, her arms turned into branches. Her hair turned into leaves. Her skin turned into bark. Her legs and feet sunk deep into the ground as roots. She turned into a laurel tree. When Apollo realized what had just happened, all he could do was to put a laurel wreath around his head. Like with the Olympians."

W<small>E DROVE AROUND THE BEACHSIDE NEIGHBORHOOD, PASSING BY</small> tourists in flip-flops and T-shirts, looking for the house. As I navigated the busy streets, avoiding the pedestrians crossing from all directions, Catherine with the map in her hand, helped me navigate.

"Two more streets down," Catherine said.

We found the woman's address right away—a two-story house with large windows and a balcony in front. To the left, sat a tall, bird of paradise tropical plant.

Catherine rang the doorbell. A woman in her late 50s with reddish hair greeted us at the door.

"Catherine, it's nice to see you again," the woman said, hugging her. "How long has it been?"

"I was still in high school the last time you visited," Catherine replied.

"I'd like to see your mom again, but I have problems with my inner ear balance. I get really dizzy when I fly."

"My friend Robert," Catherine said, turning to me.

"Robert, this is Mrs. Johnson. She stayed in my grandma's bed and breakfast one summer."

"Nice to meet you, young man."

"It's my pleasure."

Mrs. Johnson handed Catherine a large manila envelope. "Here you go. They've been here waiting for you for five days."

"Thank you," Catherine said.

"I'm not being rude, but I'm ready for my afternoon nap."

"No worries, Mrs. Johnson," I said. "We're about to have pizza."

WE PASSED BY A BEACH SHOP THAT SPECIALIZED IN TOURIST ITEMS that folks from other states, who had never seen a beach in their life, didn't mind buying. Every imaginable shell was neatly arranged on the wall, with imprints saying "San Diego" or "California."

Walking along the boardwalk, we saw beachgoers in their swimsuits laying on large, colorful towels in the sand. From a distance, men in board shorts negotiated their paddleboards in the surf. A tattooed muscle man overtly displayed his body, while sexy women in bikinis rollerbladed along the concrete pathway.

On our way to the pizza shop, we passed by some carnival games. A carnie working at a booth approached us.

"One dollar for a ball. All you have to do is knock the bottles off the stand, and you win a prize," he said, looking like somebody had knocked his teeth out with the ball he offered me.

"Do you think I should try?"

"Win something for me," Catherine begged.

I pulled out a dollar bill from my pocket and gave it to the man. I aimed at the middle of the stacked steel bottles and threw the ball hard. I heard a thump then a loud crash. All three bottles fell off the stand.

"Winner, winner, chicken dinner!" the man said, handing me my prize.

AFTER EATING AN OVERSIZED SLICE OF PEPPERONI PIZZA, I GAVE Catherine the small pink box I had won earlier. She opened it and found a silver ring with a butterfly design.

"Here," I said, placing the ring on her finger. "My promise ring to you. Luckily, I didn't get the orange ashtray shaped like a skull."

A weak smile appeared on her face. "Or the small, square mirror with shells around it."

Catherine placed her mail on the table. I watched her as she separated each envelope. Sifting halfway through the stack, I noticed her eyes grow more significant. She held a light blue envelope, her name and address handwritten. She tore it open immediately. A couple of minutes later, she placed the letter on the table.

"Is there something wrong?" I asked.

With a straight face, she said, "It's Pierre. He's coming here for graduation, and he wants me back."

"I thought you broke up with him already?"

"I did. I wrote to him a month ago, and I made it clear we were done."

"Where did you send the letter?" I asked.

"To his flat in London. It might have been lost. Looks like he's clueless."

"You gotta tell him," I said, a bit alarmed.

"This is the thing I feared the most. He's so stubborn."

"If you don't tell him now, it's going to be harder to do later on, especially when everyone's around."

With worry covering her face, she said, "I don't know what to do anymore."

"Can you call him and tell him nicely that you don't want to be with him? Write back to the return address and tell him straight that you're done with him."

"Just like that?" Catherine's voice elevated few notches. "It's not that easy. He'll probably assume that I'm just making things up to get rid of him. I know him."

"Tell him that we're together. That should settle it."

"And then what? After telling him that I'm with you, I'll be back in Andorra where all of this started, and I'll be facing the same people I'm trying to run away from. Where will you be then, Robert?" Catherine replied, looking troubled.

I tried not to think of the day when Catherine and I would eventually confront the single and most serious issue that loomed over us: our next step after graduation. I pushed the dreaded thought deep in the back of my mind where it would never surface. But like anything buried on shaky ground, issues that are not secure have a way of eventually clawing their way back to the light of day. The time had come when we needed to decide how to address the issue of how she could stay longer with me.

"I just don't want to lose you," I said.

Tears began to flow down her face. I placed my thumb on her cheek and wiped it dry.

"I don't want to be apart from you either. Why does it have to be so difficult?"

"Do you have to go back right after graduation?" I asked.

"No. But my student visa will expire soon," she said.

"Is there something we can do?"

"I can try to extend my student visa. That's all I can think of," she said.

"That would be good," I replied.

She stared at the ring on her finger, then twisted it around as if she wanted to take it off.

"Is there anything you can suggest, so I can stay here longer?" Catherine asked, desperation in her voice.

A part of me wanted to tell her to marry me. I could give her a real diamond ring instead of the one I just won. She could stay here legally forever and eventually become an American citizen. But it might make the situation worse.

Catherine put her head on my shoulder. I felt a slight wetness down the side of her face.

"I'm afraid there's even more bad news," she said. "He's coming with my parents. Now, he's gotten them involved too. My dad really likes him, and he'll try to talk some sense into me."

"This isn't an arranged marriage. If I were you, I'd return the dowry right away. It's usually 14 days with receipt and in original packaging. What's the return policy in your culture?"

Catherine laughed at my joke. "No . . . We don't do that. Besides, I already used all the gifts he gave me. I'm just afraid that he'll use everyone and everything in his arsenal to get me back."

"We'll have to prepare for that then."

"What are we anyway, Robert? We've only been seriously together for a month."

"You're the last person I think about before I fall asleep, and the first one that comes to mind when I wake up," I replied.

"I feel the same, but what does that make us?"

I looked her straight in the eye and said, "I don't want to be with anyone but you, and I don't want to label things. It sounds corny, but I think you're right. We have to make some sort of commitment between us."

"I feel the same. What should we call each other?" she asked.

"Like what? Significant other? Maybe partner? I don't really know."

"If you let me call you 'my boyfriend,' I'd be glad if you call me 'your girlfriend.'"

"Hmm . . . that sounds nice. I can introduce you as my girlfriend to my friends," I said.

Catherine moved closer and kissed me on the nose. "Does it mean we're like, you know . . . an item?"

I kissed her on the lips.

"Hey, let's forget about this Pierre crap. It'll be OK. When he comes here, I'll be there with you. My mere presence will speak louder than you telling him we're together. He'll get the idea."

"I hope you're right. He's persuasive."

"I can get pretty persuasive too, if it means protecting you."

Catherine leaned on my shoulder and hooked her arm around my neck.

"Now I'd like to celebrate."

"Celebrate what?" She replied.

"For having a new girlfriend. Don't you want to celebrate having a new boyfriend?"

"We're not in high school."

"Let's have a picnic."

"A picnic? Where?"

"I have a photo assignment tomorrow at Balboa Park. We can relax afterwards."

12

I had been half awake for five minutes when the alarm clock on my bedside table went off. As I opened my eyes, the morning light cascading from the bedroom window blinded me. I thought of the places I had to photograph in Balboa Park. They would be included in the portfolio I needed to submit to my editor. Not wanting to waste any more of the precious day, I hurried into the shower to prepare for my day with Catherine.

I closed my apartment door and strode to my car. I collapsed the MG's roof, walked to the back of the car, popped open the trunk and loaded a red cooler, a checkered picnic blanket, and my camera bag with my photo equipment: a Minolta X-700 body, telephoto and wide-angle lenses, several rolls of color slide film, a light meter, and a tripod. With everything in good order, I jumped in the driver's seat, my heart swelling in joy knowing I'd be spending the whole day with Catherine. Then I drove away.

The clean morning air uplifted me while I drove along College Boulevard. I wished that I could bottle the bliss hovering over me, so later on I could drink from it whenever I felt the presence of melancholy. The day hadn't even properly begun, yet I didn't want it to end.

The dormitory was eerily quiet when I arrived. The resident clerk that Catherine had introduced me to several months back let me through. Walking through the hallways, I noticed the usual ruckus of students talking through their open doors and running around the building was absent. It seemed like everyone was tired of either partying last night or staying up late. When I arrived at Catherine's door, I heard a muffled sound of rock and roll music drifting through the gap at the bottom of the door. I knocked. Seconds later, the music stopped. When the door opened, she greeted me with an outfit of a pink blouse and a blue jean skirt hanging just above her knees, exposing her long legs.

"Nine thirty. Right on time." I said with excitement in my voice.

"You're better than the airlines."

"I run a tight ship. Say, you look sexy," I said.

"Just for you," she replied.

She leaned forward and gave me a long, passionate kiss. I placed my hands on her hips; slowly we swayed side to side as if we were dancing. After kissing for several minutes but what felt like mere seconds, Catherine pulled away from me.

"Why don't we just stay here and lie in bed all day," I said.

She turned and sarcastically said, "And do what?"

"That thing," I replied, winking.

"But I made a bag of goodies with crackers, salami, cheese, and some sandwiches."

"I've changed my mind. Let's just picnic here."

"In the room? I'm here all the time. You have a photo contest to win," she said. "Besides, I don't like crumbs all over my bed."

"OK, fine. We'll do that thing later when you're ready."

I ENTERED THE FREEWAY ON-RAMP THAT CURVED AROUND A PATCH of grass and flowers. From her bag, Catherine pulled out a white scarf with a pink paisley design and wrapped it around her head, then donned a pair of big, white, oval-shaped sunglasses. For a moment, I imagined that we were cruising down the Amalfi Coast in a fire-red Fiat rather than in my olive green MG. I took a stick of gum from the pack, wishing it was a cigarette I just pulled out of a silver case I kept in my blazer, like a classic scene in a '60s Italian film.

I stepped hard on the gas pedal. The engine vibrated, and the speedometer's needle climbed all the way to 60 miles per hour.

"Can you go faster? This feels good," Catherine shouted through the wind noise.

"If that's what you want, I won't stop until you're satisfied." I replied, winking at her.

I PARKED THE CAR ALONG PARK BOULEVARD NEAR THE FOUNTAIN. I looked up and saw the dome of the cobalt sky above. With patches of clouds floating by, the diffused light would give my pictures less contrast. It would be a great day to take pictures.

"Will you model for me?" I asked, retrieving my camera from the trunk.

"Where's my personal chef and makeup trailer?" Catherine asked. "Just like what those super models get."

"I got them. They're all in here. It's your lucky day because your photographer also doubles as your chef," I replied, pointing to the picnic blanket and the basket of goodies.

We cut across the courtyard until reaching the Botanical Building. The brown structure stood proudly at the end of the Lily Pond.

"Lean on the banister and put your hand on your hip," I said, looking through the camera's viewfinder.

"Like this?" Catherine asked.

"Yup."

With her left leg straight, she bent her right knee, placed her hand just below her cheek and looked out in a far distance. "What about this pose?"

"Turn slightly toward the sun."

"I look like a mime. This is so ridiculous," Catherine said as she followed my instructions.

"Perfect," I said.

With a roll of film still left, I decided to use it before the day was over. Catherine and I went to the trail section of the park. The sun was beginning to dip at the horizon but still bright. I set the wide-angle lens, placed the camera a few inches from the ground, and positioned it directly in front of a yellow flower and took several shots.

"This one will make a good picture when taken at the right angle," I said, pointing to a cotton-like puffball on the ground. I picked it up and handed it to Catherine.

"What should I do with this?" Catherine asked.

"If you can just hold it up against the sun, I'll take a quick snapshot. It should create a halo effect. Kinda like the ones you see in commercials," I said, pointing the camera up to it.

Catherine blew on the puffball. The seeds scattered and floated toward the blue sky.

"Aren't we going to take a picture together?" Catherine asked.

"Let's pick that spot over there. I need a flat surface to set up my tripod."

We went around the bushes. Catherine saw a brown rabbit with its ears up, looking straight at us. "Look at that cutie," she said.

We knelt in front of the rabbit. She rubbed her thumb and

forefingers together, calling the furry animal to come toward us. I puckered my lips and made a high pitch sounds, hoping it would jump closer, so we could pet it.

"Come on."

"It's not a puppy. Making those noises won't make it come here," Catherine said.

The rabbit hopped away and disappeared into the other side of the bush.

"Oh, cutie is gone," Catherine said.

I set the camera's self-timer. Behind us, halos formed around the treetops. She hooked her arm around my hip. I placed my arm around her shoulder and pulled her close.

After an hour of picture taking, covering the buildings in the Spanish Colonial Revival style in the main promenade, the Museum of Art, the Alcazar Gardens, the Old Globe, and the California Tower, we searched for a place to picnic.

We found a shaded area away from the rest of the sightseers and near the United Nations building. I spread the red and white-checkered blanket on the green lawn and opened the picnic basket and cooler. While I uncorked a bottle of wine, Catherine sliced salami, brie, and spread a thin layer of liver pate on multigrain crackers.

"I never knew a place like this even existed," she said. "It's so peaceful."

"My secret hideout," I said, winking at her.

She offered me a plate of tasty snacks. I handed her a wine glass. A light wind shook the leaves on the trees around us, fanning a crisp eucalyptus scent. I raised my glass and said, "A toast for us."

We touched our wine glasses with a clinking sound.

"For taking me here," she replied.

We each took a sip of wine and kissed.

While we lay on the blanket and watched the sunrays flicker through the leaves above, I placed my arms under Catherine's head and pulled her closer to me.

"You know, my feet ached from walking the first night we were together," I confessed.

"Really?" Catherine said, turning toward me. "You're the one who kept talking and re-routing me. You were trying to stretch out the night, huh?"

"That obvious?" I replied.

"I was the one wearing heels."

"Did your feet hurt?"

"A bit, but your stories entertained me, and I thought you were cute."

I propped my head with my hand and looked at her.

"Did you remember anything I said?"

"No. Not really. I remember you kept looking at me."

"I couldn't take my eyes off you . . . I was wondering," I said, changing the subject, "would you like to have dinner with me?"

She rested her arm on my chest, smiled, and said, "Are you asking me out on a formal date?"

"I think fish tacos don't count. Pizza only qualifies if we're in Little Italy. Let's dress up and go to a fancy place for a nice meal. Yeah . . . you can call it a formal date."

"What are you thinking?" Catherine asked excitedly.

"Leave the details up to me. It's a surprise, and I'm sure you'll like it."

"Really? I bought a nice dress in Paris just before I came here. I'll wear that."

We cuddled on the blanket quietly and took in the enchantment of the moment. I wished that I could stretch the day a bit longer, but the hour and minute hand on my wristwatch read 6:00 p.m., and the afternoon sun had already turned the treetops a golden yellow.

13

I straightened my necktie, combed my hair back with my fingers, and took a long, deep breath. An amalgam of a hundred different scenarios on how the night with Catherine might turn out swirled in my mind. I tried to imagine how she would look in her Parisian dress. Would she like the restaurant I picked? I couldn't believe she had been my girlfriend for two months now. I felt butterflies in my stomach as I stood in front of her door. I touched the petals of the long-stemmed roses in my hand to rid myself of worry, then knocked.

"It's unlocked," Catherine said.

Catherine stood in the middle of the room when I walked in. The afternoon light streaming through the window shone on the side of her body. Her left hand dangled on her waist and right hand was on her collarbone making a small circular pattern. Her perfectly combed, champagne-colored hair hung above her shoulders. I was stunned how beautiful she looked. For a moment I thought I was looking at Botticelli's live painting of "Birth of Venus." She was wearing a long, black sleeveless dress, which showed just a small part of her cleavage; part of her thigh was peeking through the slit just above her knee. My eyes were immediately drawn to her slender legs.

I gave her the bouquet of flowers, hooked my arms around her waist and kissed her on the side of her neck.

"For you," I said, disengaging from her.

"Thank you."

She sniffed the flowers, then placed them on the desk behind her.

"You look pretty tonight," I said.

I lifted her hand above her head, and slowly she twirled in front of me.

"This is the dress I bought in Paris. Do you like it?"

"It complements your beauty, mademoiselle," I said.

"You look so handsome in your suit," she said.

"My only one."

"Where are you taking me?" she asked.

"I have everything planned. You have nothing to worry about. Just enjoy the evening," I said, reassuring her.

UNDER THE STAR-FILLED NIGHT, CATHERINE AND I HELD HANDS AS we strolled the streets of Solana Beach, a beach city north of San Diego, on the way to the restaurant for dinner. It was easy to breathe in the salty air that hung in the chilly night. The quarter moon hovering above the rooftops followed us. I could hear the ocean waves rumble a stone's throw away. We passed by the furniture shops selling tables of rare woods, art galleries with large paintings by contemporary artists, and a clothing boutique that looked more like a museum than a place to buy wearable items.

At the end of the street was a jewelry store. We stopped at the front of the store to check out the collection of artisan-crafted designs. A pendant with a face of the moon carved in glass and 10 copper spokes extending out caught my eye.

I was about to point it Catherine when I noticed her looking at the solitaire diamond rings glistening in the bright light displayed in the window.

"That would look good on your finger," I said, pointing to it.

"I love my little butterfly," she said, glancing down at her finger.

"Every woman would love to have one," I said.

"True . . . but it must come from the man she loves, or it won't mean anything," Catherine replied without taking her eyes off the ring.

I thought of bringing up the status of her student visa and how to remedy the issue. As I watched her looking at the display, I mulled over the idea of mentioning it, wondering if it was a good thing to do. She was in great spirits and timing could be perfect. Then her last words echoed in my mind. Does she love me enough that she'd be willing to defy her parents' wishes and move away from the place which she called home for all her young life?

I decided tonight wasn't the right time. I held my tongue and pushed the thought deep in the back of my mind. The time to discuss this issue is pressing but the last thing I wanted was to sour the night.

Since Catherine had been asking what food was native to California, I decided to take her to a restaurant that served California Coastal Cuisine.

The maître d', a middle-aged Hispanic man, greeted us with a warm smile. Catherine hooked her arm around mine, and we followed him. Our table was draped in a white cloth, with silverware neatly arranged. A chandelier with dimmed incandescent lights hung up above. I stole a quick glance through the large bay window overlooking the beach. The view of the sun had a warm glow. From a distance, small kids with their parents were walking along the sand, looking for smooth stones.

The maître d' pulled out Catherine's chair.

"Thank you for seating us in a great spot," I said.

"A perfect view, less than that wouldn't do," the maître d' replied, handing us menus.

About five minutes later, the waiter arrived and poured the white wine we ordered into our crystal-clear goblets.

I raised my glass and said, "To the most beautiful woman in the room."

"And to my handsome date," Catherine added.

The sound of the jazz quartet in the corner filled the dining room. A low murmur from a trumpet added softness to the ambiance. The night couldn't be more perfect. I wondered if everything happening was real. Do I deserve a night like this with a woman like her?

"Thank you for taking me here," Catherine said.

"I don't ever want to lose you." I reached for her hand and kissed it.

"I'll always be here for you, Robert." Her green eyes locked in my brown eyes.

Two waiters arrived with our appetizers. One of them presented a plate of seared bay scallops to Catherine. The other waiter placed steamed mussels in butter and garlic sauce in a copper pan in front of me.

"Sharing is how it's done," she said.

Catherine scooped mussels and broth with a large spoon onto her plate. I took a piece of the scallop. It was soft with a slight chewiness. The flavors of melted butter, squeeze of lemon, and hint of salt burst in my mouth.

"Umm . . . heavenly. You must try this," I said.

After having a piece of the scallops, Catherine set her fork down and asked, "Have you decided on the pictures you're submitting to the contest?"

"I have ten that I want to show our school editor, but now he only wants five."

"Which ones?"

"Coronado Bridge, trees from Torrey Pines, the one at Palomar Observatory, and some from Balboa Park."

"I'm excited to see your photos on display."

Our main entrée finally came. I had a filet of tuna arranged around a mound of risotto with grilled jumbo shrimp in the middle. Catherine's order: two lobster tails with a cylinder of rice pilaf sprinkled with sesame seeds.

"Bon appétit," I said, taking a bite.

It was almost midnight when we arrived back at her dorm. From a distance, we could see fire trucks with their beacons flashing and several police cruisers near the building.

"Looks like there's some excitement going on," I commented.

I parked the car on the street a few blocks away. Catherine and I got out and rushed to her dorm building. There must have been at least a hundred students in their sleepwear huddled together in the main quad. From the looks on their faces, no one seemed to be concerned with the flurry of emergency vehicles parked nearby.

"What a way to end a perfect evening," Catherine said. Frustration was written all over her face.

"This would suck if you can't get in your room tonight," I added.

We approached a group of students who were talking amongst each other. Spotting one of the girls she knew, Catherine waved to her. I immediately recognized her as the girl who lived next door to her who was initially going to take her to the museum.

"What's going on?" Catherine asked.

"Some dumbass hit the fire hydrant about an hour ago. No one is allowed in until the water department gives the OK. I heard it could take at least two hours," the girl said.

"This is a bummer," Catherine groaned.

"You can just stay at my place tonight," I said.

"Well, I can't sleep in this," Catherine replied, sounding worried. "I don't think they'll let us through even if I just wanted to get my things."

I thought of what I should do next. Catherine wouldn't leave without her things, and I certainly didn't want to leave her without knowing that she would be safely back in her dorm.

"Give me a minute. I have an idea," I said, running back to my car.

"What are you planning to do?" Catherine asked.

"I'm getting my camera."

We approached the two campus police standing next to the yellow caution tape. I remembered one of them was the officer who investigated a vandalism complaint on the campus a few weeks ago. I took a picture of the incident and convinced my paper's editor to run with the piece. He was happy with the result of my effort because several students came forward to help identify the vandal.

"Officer Martinez," I said, holding my camera to emphasize I was there on official business. "She's my assistant," pointing to Catherine. "Is it alright if we cross the line for some quick photos?"

"There's water all over the place. You might slip and fall. It's still not safe."

"This will be quick. I just need to talk to the resident clerk and ask a few details on what happened, take a few photos, then leave."

Officer Martinez lifted the yellow caution tape and let us through. "You better be fast. Get in and out. I'm timing you."

As soon as he did an about-face, we sprinted to the front entrance.

"I can't believe you pulled this off," Catherine said, giggling.

"Your apartment looks nice for a college guy" Catherine said, walking into the living room.

"Come. I'll give you a mini tour of my messy place."

"Meet my roommates, Sam and Rocket," I said, pointing to my two goldfish in the fishbowl sitting on the kitchen counter.

"Cute."

"I'll make tea to calm us down from that harrowing experience at your dorm," I said, reaching for a teakettle.

While I was turning on the stove, Catherine went to the stereo and began perusing my CD collection.

"Jimmy Hendrix, Journey, hmm . . . we might wake up the neighbors."

"This is a good one," I said, passing her the greatest love songs of the 70s CD.

A woman with an angelic voice singing softly poured out of the speakers. She turned around and looked me straight in the eyes, then placed her arms around my neck. I pulled her closer to me. Slowly, we danced to the music. She began to loosen my necktie. My hands wandered in the vicinity of her hips, then slithered up her spine until reaching her shoulder blades.

We kissed passionately as if tomorrow would never come. She worked her fingers at the top of my shirt, slowly unbuttoning each one. It felt so nice that she was in control of the situation. My shirt was half opened when the teakettle whistled from the kitchen and interrupted us.

As if being awakened from a trance, Catherine said, "Our tea."

"I'm going to throw that stupid thing out the window," I mumbled in frustration.

"You better get that before it boils over."

After finishing our cups of chamomile tea, I led her to my bedroom. A shirt was on the floor, so I picked it up and threw it in the hamper.

"You'll sleep in my bed, and I'll sleep on the couch," I said.

"Are you sure? I'm the guest." Catherine said, standing in the doorway.

"Nah . . . I'll be fine."

She stepped inside and watched me while I tore off the bed sheet from the mattress.

Standing next to the dresser, she picked up the pair of binoculars.

"You're also a bird watcher?"

"No. I use it sometimes when I'm doing some nature photography. Want to see something cool?"

I took the binoculars from her and pointed it to the pale full moon.

"I've never seen the moon this close," Catherine said, looking through the eyepiece. "Those spots look like dark bruises."

"The astronomers in the past thought they were seas and even named them."

"One of them is shaped like a lady cradling a baby."

"Really?"

I moved closer to her and looked up at the night sky.

"I'll look through one eye piece while you look through the other then I'll point to the right spot."

"Let me see," I said.

I placed my right eye on the left eyepiece and she put her left eye on the right eyepiece, then propped our elbows on the window ledge while our cheeks were pressed against each other.

"Do you see it now? I am pointing directly to it," Catherine said, reaching around my neck and pulling me even closer.

"Hmm . . . I think so. Now we need to change the bed sheet."

She stretched the garter on the clean fitted sheet. I held on to one corner while she tucked the edge under the mattress. As she changed the pillowcases, I imagined how our domestic life would be as we took care of the daily chores and the life we would build together; but that would only happen if she decided to stay with me. With the complexity of our situation—not knowing what would happen in a few months—I tried to savor the fleeting moment. I had the present moment, and that was the only thing that mattered.

I watched Catherine as she fluffed the pillows and smoothed the thin sheet with her palms. I wished she would be doing that for a very long time with me. The semester was already halfway finished and so thus, my precious time with her.

When my bedroom was ready, I went to the living room with a pillow and a blanket and prepared the couch for sleep. She went into the bathroom to change. A few minutes later, she emerged wearing an oversized T-shirt that hung all the way to her knees with no bra underneath. I could see the outline of her breasts and the curve of her hips through her thin shirt.

"Oh my, you're looking sexy tonight," I said.

"This is how I sleep. Are you sure you'll be all right on the couch? I don't want you to have a backache in the morning. I should be sleeping there."

"You're my guest."

I walked Catherine to my bedroom and kissed her goodnight.

"Thanks for the wonderful night," she said.

"You're welcome. I'll make you breakfast in the morning," I said, closing the door.

I LAY ON THE COUCH WITH THE THIN BLANKET UP TO MY CHIN. I thought of how beautiful our night had been. Having this special woman in my apartment was so lovely.

Not more than 10 minutes had passed when I heard the bedroom door open and Catherine's feet shuffling on the carpet.

"Is everything all right?" I asked.

"I couldn't sleep alone in your bed. I want you there with me."

Cupid was working overtime. I got up from the couch and followed her to the bedroom. We slid under the covers, giggling at the same time.

"Let's pretend we're camping," I said.

"There's a roof over our head. We can't exactly see the stars."

I flicked off the lamp, then reached for the inline switch connected to the star projector sitting on the nightstand. We were quiet for a moment as we watched the fake moon and stars streak across the ceiling in the dark room.

"Have you ever slept naked under the stars?" Catherine asked.

"No. But there's always a first time."

Catherine sat up, took her shirt off, and tossed it on the floor. Her impulsiveness surprised me.

"Now, it's your turn," she said, turning to me.

"I might catch pneumonia," I said, pretending to resist. "OK, fine."

She propped her chin with her hand and looked down at

me. The tips of her hair brushed against the bare skin of my chest and shoulders. I began to laugh.

"What's so funny?"

"Your hair is tickling me," I replied, pushing it away from my face.

"It's cold without clothes on," she commented.

"You need body heat." I hugged her tightly. "This skin on skin contact feels good."

Our lips found each other, and we began kissing. I felt her tongue gently slide across my lips and to my chin. I pressed her body tightly against mine, kissed her earlobe, then moved down the side of her neck.

She returned the favor by licking my Adam's apple. I kissed her neck and ran my lips along the exposed section of her back, at the same time inhaling every flowery scent of her perfume.

"Let's do this," she whispered.

"You sure?"

"Please . . . yes. Oh, yes."

At a quarter before midnight, while the stars above peeked through the partly opened window, we became one. My mind shifted into a grey zone between reason and the passion of the moment. There was no more right or wrong. No beginning and no end. There was only tonight.

14

With spring break around the corner, the mood on campus was relaxed. The students were ready for the long break and to unwind before the dreaded finals week. Some would probably go to Cabo San Lucas, a beach community at the tip of Baja California, or go on a road trip with friends.

While walking beside Catherine, I asked, "What do you want to do for spring break?"

"I haven't thought of it really," she replied.

"We could drive up to San Francisco."

"Can we stop at Monterey? Cannery Row is one of my favorite novels, then maybe swing by John Steinbeck's house. Isn't he also one of your favorite authors?"

As I considered the different options, the students playing soccer in the nearby open field caught my attention.

"We can do that."

We were near the music building when we noticed a long line snaking out the door.

"What's going on here?" Catherine asked.

"There might be some freebies. Let's check it out."

We approached the line. I was about to ask a student in jeans and a T-shirt handing out flyers when I saw Ryan and Brooke standing on the periphery.

"What's up?" I asked.

"The student symphony is playing, and the tickets are only five dollars," Ryan said.

"Let's go," I suggested.

"I might fall asleep," Ryan said.

"Come on, dear, it's only an hour. Besides, you need to expand your musical knowledge," Brooke stated.

Sitting four rows back, we watched the musicians walk to the stage. The conductor bowed, and the audience clapped. Since we arrived just in time for the performance, we were clueless about the musical program.

As soon as I heard the melodic sound of the clarinet, vibrating drums, and the horn section, I knew that I would be on a 20-minute treat. It was George Gershwin's *Rhapsody in Blue*. The music rose to a crescendo, then softened. The muted trumpet filled in the background. Catherine reached for my hand. I gave it a soft squeeze in return.

The pianist started his solo—his fingers moving fast along the keyboard. A few minutes later, like a rumble of thunder from a distant sky, the full orchestra came in like gale force winds shaking the entire auditorium. I felt the vibration of the kettledrums in my temples.

Somewhere in between, the music became playful. The main part insidiously came in like osmosis, bringing the string and horn section to a climax. Then the thunderous explosion of drums and cymbals, the downbeat of the violin bows, and the vibrato of trumpets filled the hall.

When the wonderful performance ended, the four of us walked out the door.

"What are you guys up to?" Ryan asked.

"Don't really know," Catherine answered.

"If you don't have any plans, there's something we need to talk to you about," Brooke said.

"About what?" Catherine asked.

"Do you want to go the pub across the street, so we can talk?" She suggested.

"We're thinking of someplace quieter," Brooke said.

"We can just order pizza and hang out at my place," I suggested.

"Do you have anything that's non-alcoholic?" Ryan asked.

"I have a couple of bottles of sparkling cider," I replied.

"That'll be nice," Brooke said.

"What do you think, dear?" I replied gleefully, turning to Catherine.

"Sounds nice. We can play a board game afterward," Catherine replied.

I PLACED A BOX OF ALMOND THINS AND LADYFINGERS ON THE TABLE for a snack.

"Ladyfingers for me since I'm half Italian," Catherine said, taking one of the cookies.

"Then almond thins for me since I'm half almond."

She laughed at my joke while taking a bite. "You're so silly."

Sitting at the table, while a soft music played in the background, Ryan asked, "Are we doing something for spring break?"

"We were just talking about it. We might drive up north," I replied.

"We can go to Palm Springs. I heard there's a lot of action there. Wanna go?" Brooke said.

Catherine and I looked at each other. The thought of a mini-getaway nearby sounded great.

"What's the plan?" Catherine asked.

"The plan is no plan," Ryan said.

"Eat, relax, have a good time and hang out by the pool," Brooke replied.

"I don't have a swimsuit," Catherine remarked.

"I'll take you shopping, honey," I said. "I want to see you in a sexy bikini."

The music stopped playing. I walked to the CD player and popped in my personal '80s mix.

When I returned to my seat, Catherine turned to Ryan and me, "How long have you two known each other?"

"Since our freshmen year. I've been hanging out with this dude for a long time."

"Brooke, how long have you and Catherine known each other?" I asked.

"Since we were 17. Our family took a month-long vacation in Europe one summer. Catherine's grandma ran a bed and breakfast just outside Paris and we stayed there for three nights. She happened to be staying there that summer. We bonded instantly so we hung out together every day."

"Wow, who would have thought that someone your age would be where you were staying," I said.

"We took the metro every day into the city and visited all the cafes and parks. It worked out well because it gave my parents some alone time," Brooke added.

"Tell him what happened that night," Ryan said.

Brooke was about to tell the story when the phone rang in the bedroom. I ignored it, eager to hear how things went down that day. After the fifth ring, it stopped.

"The funny thing is we ended up in the wrong bed and breakfast," Brooke said. "We were supposed to be in the one that was two streets down."

"And the rest is history, right?" I asked.

"We've been writing to each other ever since."

Ryan walked to the counter and opened a bottle of sparkling cider. He poured four glasses and set them on the table.

"About the important news we need to tell you," Brooke said, changing the subject.

"You did it!" I playfully said with a straight face. "You two won the lotto and realized college is a total waste of time."

"Please stop joking," Catherine said, squeezing my arm. "I'm getting nervous. Is the baby OK?"

"I'll let Brooke make the announcement," Ryan said.

"We're getting married two weeks after graduation. It's all set," Brooke said. Her face beaming.

"Congratulations!" I said.

"I'm happy for you two!" Catherine added.

"I'd like you to be my best man, bro," Ryan asked.

"If you could be my maid of honor," Brooke, asked turning to Catherine, "I'd be so happy."

"I would be glad to do it, but I only have one suit that I wear on all occasions though," I replied.

"You'll be in a rented tux like me. You'll be fine. All of the groomsmen will look the same."

"Then I accept the request. It would be my pleasure," I said with a big grin on my face.

"I'll be glad to be your maid of honor, Brooke," Catherine replied, blushing from the surprising news.

"What's the plan?" I asked.

"This is happening so fast. Which church and where's the reception?" Catherine interrupted.

"Brooke's cousin is helping with the planning. We'll keep you updated. All you have to do is to show up."

"May I propose a toast?" Catherine said, raising her glass. "To Ryan and Brooke."

"Yes," I added. "To the two coolest people I know."

We simultaneously raised our glasses, and each took a sip.

We had just set our cups on the counter when the phone in my bedroom rang again.

"Aren't you gonna answer that?" Catherine implored. "It might be important."

"OK, bathroom break before we play Scrabble," I said.

I got up from my chair and headed to my bedroom anticipating that a salesman would be on the other line selling me junk I didn't want to buy. Pressing the receiver to my ear, I answered, "Hello." I heard only silence at the other end. "Hello," I repeated.

I thought someone might have dialed a wrong number. Wanting to end the call right away so I could get back in the living room and join my friends, I was about to put the phone back on the cradle when I heard a familiar voice crackle in my ear. "Robert. It's me."

I didn't have to hear it again. It was the voice that had invaded my dreams for the last six months. Why wouldn't it? It had resided in the deepest recesses of my heart for several years. I felt a splinter from the past pierce my chest. My first reaction was to blurt out the words, "Oh no. Not you." The woman who had shattered my soul into a thousand pieces was on the line. Like Lazarus, who I thought had died a lifetime ago, she was resurrected. I couldn't believe she was calling me.

I cleared my throat and stood straighter, wanting to sound more formal. I moved away from the living room's direct line of sight and from Catherine's hearing distance. The last thing I wanted was to be on the phone with this woman. I didn't want anything to do with her at all. If I slammed the phone down and rushed back to the living room, I knew she'd call back. Glancing down the hallway, I was glad to see the three of them talking, clueless as to what was going on.

"Meggy, is there something I can do for you?" I asked,

keeping my voice down.

"Nothing. I just called to ask how you're doing."

I had often imagined the day we would reconnect. In my mind, it would be a few months after she broke up with me. She'd tell me that she had made a big mistake. She would apologize at a park filled with flowering cherry blossoms under the big sky. With petals scattered beneath our feet, we would hold hands. I would gaze at her eyes, blue as the ocean. Without hesitation, I'd eagerly accept her apology right away, then kiss her tender lips. As more petals fell on our hair and on our shoulders, I would forget she ever mentioned that she wanted to be away from me and tell myself that our breakup was a bad dream.

Instead of excitement, I felt cold rise from the bottom of my feet to the base of my skull. For months, I prayed that Meggy would call and take me back. But now, I had already moved on. I had Catherine now, and she was all that I wanted.

I heard footsteps coming into the bedroom. I bent backwards and peeked through the partly opened door. I saw Catherine in the hallway. I stood frozen for a second. If she heard me talking to Meggy, I would have a lot of explaining to do. She might think that I was two-timing her. Things could go south real fast. I thought of unplugging the cord from the wall if Catherine walked into the bedroom.

At the last second, she turned to the bathroom. I breathed a sigh of relief. I reached for the door and gently pushed it halfway closed.

"I'm a bit puzzled why you're calling me."

"I've been thinking about you for the past month or so and what I told you before I left. I just wanted to say . . ." Meggy said, sounding desperate.

"It's OK. If you called to say you're sorry, I forgive you. There's not much we could do. It's the past," I said, this time sounding sincere.

"I called because..."

"Aren't we done? You said so yourself before leaving." I switched the receiver to my other ear.

"I didn't leave you because I didn't want you anymore. I left because I wanted to know what was on the other side."

"What did you find out?"

"That..."

"Things didn't work out with whatever plans you had in mind."

"Didn't I tell you? I just wanted some alone time. Is that a crime? If you even cared for me, I hoped you would understand. We've been together for almost four years. Our time together must mean something?"

Her choice of words cut me deep. It was true. She cared for me deeply, treating me with love and respect.

"But you told me to move on and not to expect your return."

"I did but I also told you not to shut your heart's door if the day comes that I want to come back."

I wanted to tell her that I found someone already, and there was no hope of us getting back together again. But when I heard the bathroom door open, I panicked.

"I can't talk right now. I have some friends over. I don't think we have much to say to each other anyway."

As soon as I placed the phone back in the cradle, I turned my attention toward the door hoping Catherine didn't hear my conversation. A bullet of sweat formed on the side of my neck when the door flew open with urgency. She must have heard everything, down to the minute detail and about to confront me. With ashen face, I looked her straight in the eyes waiting for the shit storm to commence.

"We need the Scrabble set," Catherine said.

"Oh, yeah. I forgot about that," I said, relieved that she was clueless on what had just transpired.

"Is everything OK? You look like you just got off the phone with a telemarketer. They keep convincing that that you need this or that when you already told them you're not interested. It's a pain to get rid of them."

"You're right. They never leave you alone even if you've already said your goodbyes," I replied, reaching for the Scrabble set from the closet.

"Huh?" Catherine replied. Her eyebrows colliding in the middle.

As I handed her the box, I contemplated if I should come out clean and blurt out the phone call. I held my tongue fearing that it might be the wrong timing, and it could cause a big issue between us. I needed to find a way to tell Meggy not to bother me anymore because I already found someone new.

Ryan arranged the Scrabble board on the coffee table. I wanted to blurt it out and tell Catherine about the phone call, but I couldn't find the strength to do it. My eyes drifted out the window. I wanted Meggy to go away and never come back into my life, but I had a feeling that tonight's call was just a prelude for more things to come.

"Your turn, Robert," Brooke said as she handed me the bag of letters.

I randomly picked the tiles and arranged them on the rack, then quickly scanned the board. No logical words would form in my restless mind. I couldn't think of anything to put down.

"Are you OK, honey?" Catherine teased. "It's not like you're trying to come up with the solution for world peace."

"It's nothing."

A few minutes later, I put down several tiles with a low-scoring word, then I wrapped my arms around Catherine's shoulders and held her tight.

Why, after all my affairs were in order, after finding someone to love, why did Meggy come suddenly back into my life? Did she think that my feelings for her would automatically re-activate like pressing the Play button on a stereo after it's been on pause for six months. As if the song would continue like nothing had ever happened?

After we finished with the game, none of us wanted to end the night just yet. Looking in the pantry for something to serve, Catherine found a box of brownie mix.

"Let's bake this and brew a fresh pot of coffee," Catherine said.

"That'll be nice," I said numbly.

As she stirred the eggs, oil, and water with the mix to make a batter, I began to feel guilty for saying nothing about Meggy's phone call. She had been open with me about Pierre's letter. Why shouldn't I be with her? With Meggy contacting me, the tables were suddenly turned.

Confused about what to do next, I gathered the trash in the kitchen and asked, "Ryan, can you help me with this, please?"

Ryan carried the other bag, and we walked out of my apartment.

"What's on your mind? You look fidgety," Ryan asked.

"I need to talk to you about something. Remember the phone call I took in the bedroom?"

"Yeah. Anything new?"

"That was Meggy," I said.

Ryan's voice shifted to a serious tone. "What does she want?"

"I don't really know."

"Out of the blue, she's phoning you? I bet she wants to get back together with you."

"As far as I'm concerned, we have nothing to talk about."

"Tell her you found someone new."

"I told her we're done, but she sounded as if she was in

denial."

"Then call her back tomorrow."

"I don't know her phone number in New York."

"That's a problem."

"Should I tell Catherine?"

"If you tell her about Meggy, she might think that . . . well, you know. It's too risky."

"I don't want to get back together with her, period," I replied, shaking my head.

"I know that, bro. Catherine will probably think Meggy wants you back. It can backfire, and she could start resenting the fact that Meggy is still around."

"Dude, I don't want to be with her anymore. It's that simple," I said.

"As soon as Meggy calls you back, don't beat around the bush. Tell her straight that you found someone new, and it would be better if she stopped calling you. Problem solved. This issue will all go away sooner than you think."

I realized how difficult it would be to tell Catherine about the call, but I didn't want any complications. Catherine was already worried about Pierre showing up soon. If I told her about Meggy's call, things could get complicated.

"Why's Meggy coming back into my life? Why now? She broke my heart last time we were together."

"Who knows? Maybe her grand New York adventure didn't work out. Maybe she didn't find 'Mr. Tall, Dark, and Handsome' and was calling to patch things up. What's your plan with Catherine anyway?"

"I want to ask her if she'd like to stay here longer and live with me, but it's complicated."

"Are you two done after graduation?"

"That's not what I want."

"Just leave it be for now. I don't think Meggy will call back."

15

With graduation peeking around the corner, I began to seriously think about what to do about Catherine's immigration status. I knew the day would come when we would have to confront the single and most significant issue that surrounded our relationship—how we would proceed after graduation. It was fun and games in the last three months, but if I didn't come up with a concrete plan on how we would stay together, I might as well say my goodbyes now. Because now, we're heading that way.

We needed to talk about our next step. Her student visa would expire a month after school ended. I couldn't bear the thought of her moving back to Andorra. I could suggest that she apply for a master's program and that could do the trick for a couple of years, but I doubt if she wanted to do that. She mentioned that she'd been going to school nonstop since she was a toddler and was glad that this was the final year. She could also apply for a work visa. There should be plenty of employers who would be probably hire Catherine for her accounting skills, but she also mentioned she wanted to travel before getting into the workforce.

The only viable option for her to stay permanently in the U.S. was if she married an American citizen. It was the nuclear option, and since we were only 22, that was the furthest thing from our minds. Asking her to be my fiancée would probably send her running for the hills. Besides, that was the reason why she came here in the first place—to get away from Pierre and the prospect of life in domesticity. We weren't ready to get married. I wondered if Catherine was also thinking of how she could stay in the States longer. She said she wanted to be with me, and she loved living in San Diego, but I had no idea how we were going to do that.

I picked up my backpack from the floor. As I headed to the door, I heard the phone ring. Hoping Catherine was calling me, I grabbed the receiver and placed it to my ear.

"Hello."

"Robert, it's me."

Hearing Meggy's voice, I resented her for calling me again, but at the same time, I felt a sense of relief, so I could tell her to leave me alone.

"Meggy, is there anything I can help you with? Is there any reason we should talk?" I asked with a stern voice.

"Robert, I know I've made mistakes, but all I'm asking for is the two of us to know each other again. I now understand how badly I hurt you."

"I thought we were done."

"There are important matters I need to tell you."

"Like what?" I thought about saying "Unless you're going to tell me we have a baby together," but I decided against it.

"A lot has happened when I was away. I just want us to be friends like before, and maybe . . . maybe we could start over."

"Meggy, you hurt me deeply when you decided to leave. I dealt with the pain as best as I could. I cried about it. I'm over that now. I've forgiven you for whatever happened in the past. I don't want you to go to bed every night thinking I hate you. We had a great four years together. Is that what you want to hear from me?"

"I'm glad you said that," she replied.

I sensed the relief in her voice. I was about to tell her that I was involved with someone else when she said, "I just want to clear the air between us when we meet."

"Meet when?" I asked puzzled.

"I sent five of my paintings to the fundraiser for the Women and Children's Shelter. I saw your name on the invitation as one of the artists who submitted an entry. I'll be flying to San Diego during spring break."

I was speechless with the bomb she dropped on my lap. How could she do this to me now? I'm not her puppy that she could leave in one corner and expect to be jumping for joy as soon as she opened the front door. Shocked with her revelation, all I could do was to stare at the phone, stunned with the thought of the impending face-off between us.

As soon as my history class was over, I closed my textbook and hurried out the door wanting to talk to Ryan.

Students were streaming from spaces between the buildings, anxious to get to their next classes. I passed by a couple of them handing out flyers. One of them tried to talk to me, but I waved her off. To my right, the library was bright in the late morning sun. With wheels clicking on the gaps between the concrete, a student on a skateboard almost rolled over my toes. I could see the planetarium's silver dome grazing the gray marine layer hovering up above. I made my way toward a row of benches next to the administration building hoping to find Ryan. He wasn't there.

Pulse quickening, beads of perspiration rolling down the

side of my face, I held onto my backpack straps to prevent it from swinging side to side. I walked past two girls; the coconut smell of sunscreen wafted in the air. I wished I was at the beach instead of worrying about how to solve my dilemma with Meggy.

Desperate for where to find him, I headed to the newspaper office.

The office was empty when I arrived. Not knowing where to go next, I picked up the phone sitting on the desk and dialed.

"Hello."

"Hey, buddy, it's me," I said, relieved he was home.

"What's up? You sound hurried. Got nice pictures?"

"A few. Hey, listen, I just spoke to Meggy again. She submitted some of her paintings to the fundraising event. She's flying out and seems excited to meet me."

"Uh oh. What are you planning to do?" Ryan asked.

"I really don't know."

"She'll definitely see Catherine and it'll be World War III."

"That's why I'm calling you. I can't sweep this under the rug anymore. I think it's better if I just skip the event," I said.

"I'll be there writing about it, and Brooke is coming. Catherine is excited to see the pictures you've taken. You have no valid reason to skip it. What if you won? Who's going to accept your prize? Alejandro worked hard to get your pictures included in the auction, and if he doesn't see you there, he will be pissed."

"If I don't show up, there will be no chance I'll see Meggy."

"Brooke will be there and Meggy knows her. Brooke will tell Catherine about her. Meggy will ask about you when they meet and introduce herself as your ex. It will be an awkward situation for the three of them. Catherine would probably blow a gasket; then you're screwed, big time."

"What if I tell Catherine that I'm not interested in going?"

"And what are you going to tell her? That your ex-girlfriend is going to be there, so you're planning to skip town? Just face the music and come clean. Just tell her the truth that Meggy had called you. You have no choice."

"I guess I'll come up with something like I have a toothache. Catherine is already stressed. Her ex-boyfriend is coming here for her graduation. If I tell her about Meggy . . . I don't know how she'll react."

"If you don't tell her now, bro, you'll have a bigger mess later."

I hung up the phone and processed Ryan's advice in my head. It made sense. Regardless of what course of action I took, there would be repercussions.

BAFFLED WITH THE QUICK TURN OF EVENTS, I LEFT THE CAMPUS TO work on my next assignment at Mission Trails Regional Park.

Standing next to a large rock, I gazed at the open field and marveled at the big blue sky. The cloud formations looked like smoke signals rising behind the treeless, brown mountains in the distance. I followed the trail looking for a place to photograph, passing by knee-high bushes, as the gravel made crumbling sounds beneath my feet. I came across a clump of trees so tall that they seem to be reaching up to the stratosphere.

I followed a stream gushing over moss-covered rocks until I stumbled upon the Old Mission Dam. I screwed a polarizing filter into the camera lens to cut away the stray reflections, so the sky would even look bluer. I took several pictures.

Sitting on the stone wall, I placed my camera on my lap, pointed it toward the running stream and set the shutter on low speed. I took several shots hoping to create a feather-like effect while the water gushed through the dam's opening. An eddy in the stream had trapped a floating leaf. For some reason, it reminded me of my situation with Meggy. I didn't have a clue of what to do with her. I picked up a stick lying on the ground and pushed the leaf free. I wished I had a stick that I could wave like a magic wand at my seemingly dire situation, so I could push my worries away and let the downstream current carry them to some faraway place where they could no longer catch up to me.

A lump formed in the pit of my stomach. I had a feeling the issue wouldn't go away quietly. Telling Catherine about Meggy seemed like the only way to solve it. I was confident she'd understand.

CATHERINE WAS LYING ON HER BED READING WHEN I WALKED INTO her room. I sat next to her and kissed her on the top of her head.

"What's going on? Are you going to tell me you aren't going to *Les Miserables* with me?"

"It's about . . ." I said, unsure how I should break the news.

"The show is sold out, and you cannot get tickets."

"I don't think they're on sale yet."

I smiled at her attempt to lighten the mood.

Clearing my throat, I said, "Remember that call I took in my bedroom when we were playing Scrabble at my apartment?"

"Yeah, now that you mention it. How much do you owe to the bill collector?"

"That was Meggy trying to reconnect with me."

"What does she want?" she asked, concern in her voice. "Does she want to get back together with you?"

"I told her straight up that I am not interested in getting back together. Or anything close to that."

"Why are you telling me this?"

"Meggy will be at the fundraiser. She submitted some of her paintings for the art auction. I don't want you to be surprised if you see her."

"And you're planning to do what?"

"Bring a sharpie and mess up her paintings. Look, I don't know. I'd like you to stay very close to me, so she'll know right away we're together. The same game plan when Pierre comes here."

Catherine looked out the window as if searching for an answer.

"Seems like we can't escape our pasts."

"I don't want her in my life. You know that."

Catherine put her hand on my face, and said, "How come these things are happening to us? First, it's Pierre, now her."

"Why don't we just run away together? Away from everybody."

"We can't. I've done that already, and I can't run far enough," she replied.

"I just don't want you to get overwhelmed with everything that is coming at us."

With a tender smile, Catherine replied, "Robert, we care deeply about each other; it's going to be OK."

"I'll trust you on this one," I said, feeling relieved.

16

After more than two hours cramped in Brooke's car, we finally arrived in Palm Springs. Spring break had finally arrived, and I was glad for the respite. The semester was about three quarters finished and quickly coming to a close. With this being my last spring break, I wanted to enjoy each minute before it became a footnote to my college days.

To my far right, I could see houses with long, sloping roofs and aquamarine, rectangular swimming pools, probably owned by some big shots in Hollywood. We turned onto the main street, lined in palm trees with shops and restaurants on either side. I rolled down the window, surprised but not shocked to see college students jamming the streets in their shorts and bikini tops. We followed the cars in front of us and slowly inched forward.

"Look at that crazy guy," Ryan pointed to a rollerblading muscleman wearing only a Speedo.

After an agonizing half hour, we arrived at the resort where we'd be staying at for the next two nights. Built in the '60s, the hotel reflected the presence of Hollywood stars who stayed here not so long ago. We gathered our things and headed straight to the reception desk. A young woman who only looked a couple of years older than us checked our IDs, then issued our room keys.

I glanced to my left. The pool area was half full of students hanging around with drinks in their hands. The party had already started even before our arrival. Wanting to chill and some alone time, we proceeded to our room while Ryan and Brooke went the other way.

"See you in two hours," Ryan shouted as he disappeared at the end of the hallway.

Our room was spacious and bright. We could see the tall palm trees and Mt. San Jacinto in the far distance.

"It's so pretty here," Catherine said, diving onto the bed.

I lay next to her and kissed her on the cheek. "I love these pillows. They're like clouds under my head."

"I could stay here forever with you," Catherine said with a sweet sigh.

She wrapped her legs around my thigh and placed her arm across my chest. I stared at the ceiling fan spinning slowly, then placed my arm under Catherine's head. The light breeze blowing through the window and the peacefulness in the room began to chip away at my exhaustion from the trip. I turned to Catherine wanting to whisper in her ear how much she meant to me, but her eyes were already closed. Not wanting to interrupt her deep slumber, I gently pushed her yellow hair off my neck and turned toward the window. The clouds slowly drifted, changing their shapes every so often. A few minutes later, I fell asleep.

THE NOISE FROM THE STUDENTS PARTYING AT THE POOL WOKE ME up. I checked the clock sitting on the nightstand. It was almost 4:00 p.m.

Nudging Catherine on the shoulder, I said, "Wake up. We've been sleeping for an hour and a half."

"I don't want to go anywhere. I just want to stay here," she said, rubbing her eyes.

"They're probably downstairs already."

Catherine got out of bed and walked straight to the bathroom. I put on a pair of light blue board shorts and a T-shirt. Ten minutes later, Catherine emerged from the bathroom wearing a pink, two-piece swimsuit with black polka dots. From her overnight bag, she pulled out a white transparent cover-up.

"Let's go," she said. "I'm ready."

I picked up the towels resting on the chair and opened the door. Catherine reached for my hand, and we linked our fingers. As we headed outside, I wondered what the afternoon had in store for us.

If the pool area was about fifty percent full when we arrived, it was now close to eighty percent.

"Where are they?" Catherine asked, looking through the throngs of people in front of us.

With everyone looking nearly all the same in their poolside attire, it was difficult to find Ryan and Brooke. Not knowing where to look, I took Catherine's hand and led her through the thick crowd, careful not to lose her. Most of the guys were shirtless and held beer bottles while trying to impress the girls sipping on wine coolers.

After combing through every inch of the pool area, I spotted Ryan wearing Hawaiian swim trunks and Brooke in a black and yellow, one-piece swimsuit lying on the poolside recliners.

"Whassup?" I asked.

"Catchin' some sun," Brooke replied.

"Sorry we're late," Catherine said, "We took a quick nap."

Brooke looked at us and said, "A quick nap, huh? I'm guessing that's not all you did."

"A gentleman never kisses and tells," I said, smiling. "What are we drinking tonight?"

"Iced tea," Ryan said.

"Long Island Iced Tea?" Catherine asked.

"No. Just an old-fashioned, Southern style sweet tea with lemon and mint," Ryan said.

"We're taking a break on the alcohol. Bad for the baby," Brooke added.

Ryan poured our drinks, then handed us tall, skinny glasses.

I said, "To the four of us."

"To the four musketeers," Catherine followed up.

We touched our glasses and sipped our drinks.

"Wow. This is good." Ryan said.

After we finished the pitcher of iced tea, I signaled to Catherine with my eyes and pointed to the pool with my lips.

"We're gonna check out the water," I said.

She handed me sunscreen and said, "Apply some on my back."

With the palm of my hand, I evenly spread the lotion making sure that I covered most of her exposed skin. With the sweet smell of jasmine drifting into my nose, it immediately put me in a festive mood.

I turned around and said, "Now, my turn."

Catherine squeezed a thin line on the back of my neck and my upper shoulders. Gently, she massaged the lotion into my skin. Confident that we were protected from the harsh ultraviolet rays, we jumped in the pool, ready to soak in the desert sun.

With the sun dissipating behind the mountains, I began to feel thirsty. We'd been in the pool long enough, so we decided to get out of the water before our fingers got pruney.

"Let's get a drink," I said, swimming to the makeshift bar at the end of the pool.

Catherine leisurely swam next to me, breaststroke style. When we reached the bar, she scanned the different bottles of rum and vodka, looking confused at which drink to order.

"I like those drinks that come in a cute glass," she said.

I waved to the bartender. When he approached me, I asked him to give Catherine a tropical drink and something colorful for me. A few minutes later, he handed her a Mai Tai with a wedge of pineapple on the rim and a tiny umbrella poking out. My drink, a tall tequila sunrise, was orange on top and red at the bottom with an orange wedge and cherry on a toothpick.

"Cheers," I said, raising the glass.

With the pool almost at maximum capacity with spring breakers, the DJ at the far end began to spin. The noise level from the electronic dance music blasting from giant speakers and everyone talking made it difficult for me and Catherine to hear each other. I could tell that most of the partygoers were drunk. From the deep end of the pool, a guy in black swim trunks cannonballed. A loud cheer erupted. Water splashed all over, and some of it landed in my drink. In a different time, I would have complained, but I didn't mind. Getting splattered, stepped on and being bumped was part of the fun.

"Let's dance!" Catherine yelled through the loud music at the same time tugging my arm.

We got out of the water. As we made our way into the middle where everyone was gathered by the speakers, I shouted, "Excuse me!" in a tiny space between a group of people. No one seemed to care, or they were flat out ignoring me, so I decided to carry her in my arms.

"We're going to fall," she said.

In a deep voice, trying to imitate a radio announcer, I said, "I already fell for you."

"Cheesy," she said as she pinched my neck, "but you scored big points on that one."

Next thing I knew, we were squeezing ourselves through the crowd and into the middle of the makeshift dance floor. The strobe lights pulsated from the corners, and the red and blue lights flickered. A surge of energy filled me as the electric lights supercharged the night and the low pulsating bass thumped right through my chest. Catherine swung her hips from side to side, swinging her arms freely and in unison with a trumpeter in a blue Hawaiian shirt, who played along with the DJ. We were lost in the moment of the vibrating music and the buzz of alcohol. I followed the rhythm of the beat and made a move as if I was raising the clouds above me.

I felt a tap on my shoulder. When I turned, I saw Ryan and Brooke dancing next to us.

"Glad you found us!" I said, shouting through the loud music.

Everyone within a 100-foot radius was between 21 and 25 years old. For the first time in years, I felt as if I didn't have a care in the world.

Catherine wrapped her arms around my neck. "Thank you for taking me here."

I wondered if I was in a dream. It felt so easy being with Catherine, the woman I'd fallen in love with, my best friend Ryan, and the woman he'll be marrying soon. I savored the night, wishing time would stand still where there wasn't any school or any responsibility in the world. It was one of those stolen days, and I tried to sear each passing second into my mind. Like being on a boat passing through a breathtaking fjord, I knew deep inside that tonight would never be repeated. After Ryan and Brooke got married, they'd be in full swing with their domestic life. Ryan would soon find a career, and Brooke would be busy raising their child.

I didn't know what the future held for Catherine and me. But as for now, I was in paradise with a woman tailor-made for me. I thought of my anthropology instructor's lecture a few years ago—some cultures believed that the dream state is reality and life on earth is but a dream. It did not matter where I was in the moment. This was the place where I belonged and where I wanted to be.

I glanced at the purple blue sky and savored the moment, realizing how lucky I was to have a woman like Catherine and friends like Ryan and Brooke.

We were in the prime of our lives. The thumping bass and the uplifting synthesizer filled the desert sky.

I didn't want the music to end as we danced the night away.

17

I arrived at the Swinging Leaf Winery where the auction was being held with a myriad of thoughts swirling in my mind. The mountain wind blowing from the east cooled my nerves, but it couldn't take away my worries as I anticipated how the night would turn out. I checked my reflection in the rearview mirror, making sure that nothing looked out of place. Satisfied, I got out of the car and headed toward the reception area.

Though I had arrived half an hour early, the place was already half full. I noticed a mixture of people from their early 20's to late 50's gathered in the grassy area under the parasol of stringed incandescent lights. Certain that Catherine, Ryan, and Brooke would be among the crowd, I headed in that direction right away. I craned my neck and swept my immediate area, checking for any sign and expected that I'd stumble upon them. But they were nowhere in sight. They should've already arrived. I checked my watch but instead of the time registering in my head, the pulse pounding in my throat distracted me.

I thought of the scenario Catherine and I had planned. We'd be together and hold hands all night so that Meggy and the whole world wouldn't doubt that we were a serious couple. The gears in the machine of our plan were well-oiled; all I needed to do was to go through the motions of the night's festivities. My plan was simple but effective. I would introduce Catherine as my girlfriend when Meggy approached us, and that should settle any doubts once and for all.

The art patrons were chatting among themselves, admiring the paintings, sculptures and photographic prints, sipping wine, and munching on cheese and crackers. I walked through the display area and saw the pictures I'd taken resting on several easels: Coronado Hotel with its red sloping roofs and the bottom of Scripps Pier with waves crashing on concrete pylons. A tiny smile appeared as I was honored to have my prints included in the art auction.

I thought of how I'd react when I came face-to-face with Meggy. I wondered if she was still attractive the way I remembered her. Would she still have dark, shoulder length hair? I remembered that she would spend extra minutes combing and curling it whenever I came to pick her up at her house before going on a date. Though Meggy told me she wanted to see me again only as friends, Ryan's warning had some truth. I was sure that she wanted to get back together with me; otherwise, she wouldn't have flown all the way here from the East Coast for an art event.

I searched the immediate area for Catherine again. Still, she wasn't around.

The bidding started. The people interested in the artwork placed their bids on clipboards next to the paintings, photographs, or sculptures they wanted to take home. I checked my watch again. It was precisely 7:00 p.m. Catherine, Ryan, and Brooke should have arrived 15 minutes ago. I thought of calling them, but figured they were already on the road.

My sight wandered toward a group of women in formal eveningwear, standing next to a sculptor. My jaw dropped when

I saw Meggy by the wine bar, talking to some of the fundraising supporters of the fundraising. She wore a dark blue pencil skirt that complemented her deep blue eyes, with an off-white, off-the-shoulder blouse. Even I had to admit that she looked good. I searched my immediate vicinity and prayed that Catherine would soon appear. This turn of events was just short of disastrous. The timing was wrong. Engaging in a chummy conversation with her without Catherine present was the last thing I wanted to happen. Wanting to immediately change location so Meggy wouldn't be able to spot me, I ducked behind the people in front of me and hurried away. When I finally made it far enough and out of her line of sight, I finally breathed a sigh of relief.

I muttered under my breath, "If only I could find Catherine, I'd be set."

Thinking that it would be the best way to avoid running into Meggy in an untimely manner, I hurried to the winery's front entrance to meet Catherine as soon as she arrived.

I had just reached the double doors when a voice called out to me: "There you are."

It sounded like Meggy. A tiny bead of sweat rolled down my forehead, dreading that Meggy had found me. If she did, it was the worst place to be. Catherine was about to arrive, and I didn't want her to see us alone together. Fearing the worst, I turned around.

I was so glad to see the event organizer, Mrs. Anderson. Whew!

"Robert," she said with a smile, "Are you enjoying the night?"

"Ah, yes," I said.

"Your photos have some high bids. Looks like you're going to win some money."

"That's great," I said, wanting to wiggle my way out of the conversation.

"Wanna try some white wine? I'm on my way to the bar."

"I'm going to my car to get something," I lied. "Can I meet you there?"

Mrs. Anderson shrugged her shoulders as if saying it was my loss because the wine was free. She walked away without saying anything further.

After waiting more than ten minutes standing by the entrance, I started to worry that something might have happened. I decided to look for a payphone and call Ryan's home hoping his roommate would answer and tell me when he left. I was relieved to see there was one near the public restroom. I was reaching for the receiver when I stopped in my tracks. Meggy stood a few feet away wearing a debutante smile. My heart sank. I wondered if she expected me to jump into her arms and let bygones be bygones. I stood frozen and didn't say a word.

"Hi, Robert," Meggy said, twirling her hair.

For the first time in months, I stood an arm's length away from the woman who had captured and then broken my heart. I could still remember the first time I met her during my freshman orientation day. During the lunch break, the only seat available was next to her. Seeing that I was carrying a tray of food, she waved at me and invited me to join her. The minute Meggy introduced herself, I immediately felt the warmth of her smile. Over lunch, she confessed that, since she was from Colorado, she had never seen the green flash during sunset. So, afterwards, I drove her to one of my favorite spots in Encinitas. Sitting on a bluff, we talked while we waited for the sun to disappear on the horizon. As soon as the flash of green appeared on top of the setting sun, simultaneously, we turned toward one another. The spark lit up the natural attraction between us. We were inseparable ever since.

But that was in another life. A page in my book that had already been ripped away and lost in yesterday. Tonight, I had more pressing matters I needed to tell her.

"It's been a long time," I said as my eyes searched for Catherine's presence.

Meggy, never one for small talk, said what was on her mind.

"Can I honestly tell you why I'm here tonight?"

"What's on your mind?" I asked, pretending I was clueless.

"Robert, I'm sorry about the terrible things I've done to you. Things are..."

I stopped her mid-sentence and said, "Meggy, it's the past... It's OK. Feelings change. People change. Like I told you on the phone, I'm not angry anymore."

A few seconds of silence followed.

"I'm happy you feel that way," she replied, her face lighting up. "That means a lot to me."

With no hope that Catherine would arrive soon and to avert further disaster, I decided to tell her that I was already dating someone and that staying away from me to avoid any complications would be the best for both of us.

"Meggy, there's something you should know. We can't..."

Mrs. Anderson interrupted us.

"The bids have been tallied, and the winners will be announced. All participating artists must stand by the stage," she said, putting her hand on our backs and nudging us to move forward.

"I think we need to be there. Hold that thought," Meggy said, letting out a sigh.

"I guess I'll see you later," I replied, stepping away.

The art patrons and the guests who sponsored the event stood on the grassy area facing the stage, waiting for the presentation to begin. Mrs. Anderson walked onto the stage and said, "I've been hosting this auction for four years. Tonight, we had record donations. Thanks to the student artists who participated, our grand total in pledges is . . . drum roll, please . . . $10,000."

The crowd erupted in cheers.

"Ever since the auction began, we have awarded the top three artists with a certificate of appreciation and $300 in prize money."

The talons of worry gripped me. I began to fret the fact that something horrible might have happened to Catherine, Ryan, and Brooke. As the awards ceremony continued, I couldn't pay much attention to what she was saying. At that point, I didn't care if I won anything. I just wanted Catherine by my side.

"For the fundraising benefit for the year 1990, the winning artists are Meggy O'Brien for painting, John Cohen for sculpture, and for photography, Robert . . ."

Loud claps erupted from the audience.

"Will those three people please come to the stage?" Mrs. Anderson requested.

I scanned my surrounding for the last time hoping to see some friendly faces, but there was no trace of any of them.

I didn't want to be alone with Meggy.

Flashes popped in my face, blinding me. I had just stepped onto the stairs that led up to the stage when I felt Meggy's arm curling around mine. I thought to myself how out of touch she was. I tried to gently pull away, but with her excitement, her grip tightened. I was horrified with the thought that everyone would think we were a couple winning a prize together.

The other winning artist, John Cohen, who wasn't paying attention while walking, unintentionally wedged himself between us. Meggy suddenly loosened her vise-like grip on me. Immediately taking advantage of the luck that landed in my lap, I gently pulled my arm off of her and pretended to shake the hand of one of the organizers on the stage while freeing myself.

I stood on stage with at least eight people and listened to the speaker thank everyone for attending the night's festivities and donating to a good cause. I squinted and scanned the audience through the bright lights directed in my face, but couldn't see anything through the glare.

The host presented our certificates and prize monies. Meggy turned to me and said sweetly, "Congratulations, Robert. You're a great photographer and won't be relegated to a life of doing weddings and company events. Your work might be in *National Geographic* someday."

"Thank you," I said.

With one fluid motion, she pulled me toward her and gave me a kiss on the lips. I thought to myself, "From all the places she had to do this, why here in the middle of the stage for the entire world to see." I prayed that Catherine didn't see the stunt she pulled and wanted to shout at her. "What are you trying to do?"

"Robert, remember our agreement to be together again after six months of separation. I still want you, and I want us to be together again," she said loudly through the cheering crowd.

Ever so gently, I pushed her away from me. I noticed the fruity smell of alcohol on her breath. I told myself, "That's it. I'm out of here." As soon as I freed myself from her, I turned to the side of the stage for my quick escape. To my shock, I saw Catherine standing about 20 feet away from me behind several people. A look of disbelief painted on her face. I was sure she heard what Meggy said. I felt as if the gazebo's roof had collapsed on top of me. Meggy's playful kiss and drunken proposal screwed up the night. The stage felt as if it was on fire. I wanted to jump off and run to Catherine right away—to tell her that Meggy kissed me and that I didn't initiate it.

As I hurried down the stairs, the event photographer placed his hand on my shoulder and said with an impatient tone, "I need to take your pictures with the other artists and organizers."

"There's someone I need to get to . . ." I replied frantically.

"This will be a quick one. Come on, Robert," one of the organizers said. "We're waiting."

Not wanting to be rude, I turned back.

I stood on the stage and waited for the art patrons and donors who were taking their sweet time to join us while my heart rate quadrupled with each passing minute. The snail's pace of pausing and smiling for the pictures hacked away the precious seconds I needed to get to Catherine. I felt the photographer was the cruelest person on earth for taking his time, arranging us for the perfect shot. Time ticked by slowly. I forced myself to smile even as I raged inside.

After 10 minutes that seemed like an eternity, the photo shoot finally ended. I hurried to the grassy area, furiously looking for Catherine and squeezing my way through the wine-soaked crowd.

I frantically searched each section of the winery, checking each face like a mother who had lost her only child. Fear churned in my stomach. I couldn't believe that the perfectly planned evening had turned into a total nightmare.

I felt a ray of hope when I saw Ryan standing in the bar area with a glass of wine in his hand.

"Where's Catherine?" I asked, out of breath.

"Dude, she took off with Brooke," Ryan said, taking a swig of his drink.

"What the heck happened? You're all late," I said.

"I heard a noise in my car's engine, and I didn't want to risk breaking down on the side of the road, so I switched cars with Brooke."

"Where are they?" I asked.

"Catherine saw everything, dude. She was so upset she asked Brooke to take her back to the dorm. They left me here."

"It's not how it looked," I said, my voice cracking.

"I knew this sort of thing would happen. Let's get out of here. You need to see her now to prevent a total meltdown," Ryan said, placing the glass on the table.

Not wanting to waste another minute, Ryan and I jumped in the car and sped off from the winery's parking lot.

NEXT THING I KNEW, THE WIND WAS BLOWING HARD IN MY FACE, and my knees shook out of control. I didn't remember how I got on the freeway, but it didn't matter because all I wanted was to get to Brooke's apartment like right now, but I couldn't get there fast enough. I dug my fingernails into the steering wheel out of frustration. My body felt numb, and my head throbbed as if it was going to explode. Everything was falling apart, like a house made of straw in the middle of a storm.

Just an hour before the event started, I was excited, anticipating that I might win some cash, and I was so proud of myself that people might actually buy my photographs. I was on top of the world. I was even smiling as I tied my tie like in a shaving commercial. Soon, I'd be spending time with good friends and the woman I loved. Life didn't get much better than that. Now, I was breaking the speed limit, and the tie around my neck choked me. I ripped it off and chucked it on the floor. I glanced down at the speedometer, the needle pointed to 80 mph. I imagined driving a four-door sedan and Brooke was with us, just in case the Highway Patrol stopped us. I could easily explain that we're taking her to the hospital to have the baby checked to avoid a speeding ticket . . . but that only works in the movies. I wanted to speed up, hoping to get to Catherine as soon as possible, but my car could only go so fast. The freeway in front of me went on for miles, as lengthy as the regret I felt for not pushing Meggy away from me.

We arrived at Brooke's apartment a little past 9:00 p.m. From the parking lot, I could see the light from her bedroom window. I pushed open the door. I was about to jump out and run to the front door when Ryan stopped me.

"Wait here. I need to talk to Brooke alone first," Ryan said, getting out of the car.

I felt sick to my stomach with the thought that Catherine would probably not want to talk to me. How could I blame her for my carelessness?

Five minutes later, Ryan emerged from the apartment with a serious look on his face.

"She's at her dorm. Go now, and leave me here," Ryan instructed.

I shoved the gearstick into first, stepped hard on the gas pedal and peeled out, begging the gods to help me say the right words to get Catherine back. I prayed that she would find it in her heart to understand that there wasn't anything going on between Meggy and me.

I parked the car outside the dorm and got out. As I ran across a small patch of garden, I imagined the shit storm waiting for me. I wondered if Apollo felt the same as he chased Daphne through the forest.

The resident clerk, who I'd become friendly with during my frequent visits, greeted me when I arrived at the lobby.

"Robert, what are you doing here so late?"

"Sally, I'm here to see Catherine," I said.

"No visitors are allowed after 9:00 p.m. You know that."

"I just need to talk to her. It's crucial. I won't be long," I said in a pleading tone.

She looked at me with suspicious eyes. "Is everything OK? She ran up to her room crying."

"That's why I'm here. There's been a bit of a misunderstanding between us."

She paused for a moment. With a puzzled expression, she looked as if contemplating if she should let me through.

I leaned closer and whispered, "Please, we had a horrible night, and I need to make things right."

With the possibility of not being allowed in, I thought of my next step. I could walk outside, shout to her window and cause a big commotion until she came out. Just as the resident clerk warned me that she'd call the police for public disturbance if I didn't stop, I'd see Catherine striding down the stairs toward me. I would kneel in front of her and beg for forgiveness. She would run her fingers through my hair like she'd done in the past and tell me to forget the terrible night had ever happened. We would passionately kiss and hold each other with pure affection.

"I don't want to break the rules. I don't think I can let you in," giving me a sly wink.

"I'm guessing you've been in love before, and you understand how complicated these feelings are."

"I understand. A lover's quarrel must be mended right away. Good luck," she said, letting me through.

I STARED AT THE STRIP OF LIGHT ESCAPING UNDER THE DOOR imagining Catherine in bed with her head buried in several pillows. I gently knocked, not sure if she would even open the door. There was no answer. Wanting to know what was going on inside, I pressed my ear against the hollow door. I couldn't hear even her breaths. The room seemed empty. After a few minutes standing in the hallway with no acknowledgment of my presence, I decided to turn the doorknob. To my surprise, the door opened. Through the faint light from the small lamp, I saw the flowers I had given her a week ago. The petals were dry and barely hanging on the frayed stems. One blow from the wind and they would crumble on the top of the desk. The dead flowers mirrored my situation, hanging in the balance.

I walked in and checked the space in between the walls and bed. I was disappointed to find that she was gone.

Not wanting to give up my search, I walked out of the building worried where she went. She couldn't have gone too far. Feeling sick to my stomach, I started to blame either the stress of not finding her or the cheese cubes I ate while dodging Meggy.

I searched the immediate area, hoping she was out on a walk for some fresh air. After more than 15 minutes of frantic search, I concluded that it would be better if I returned early in the morning to explain my side of the story. As I was heading back to my car, I heard muted sobs coming from a bench near a tree. Catherine sat by herself, bent forward beneath the jaundiced halogen light.

I slid next to her.

She sat up and turned her eyes soaked with tears to me.

"It's not what you think," I meekly said. "I didn't know she'd kiss me like that and say what she said. She means nothing to me. You were supposed to be there, so she'd know I'm with you."

"I saw everything that went down. It didn't matter if I was late or if I didn't make it. You should know what to do. What if Pierre leaned in to kiss me, I'd push him away. No matter how awkward that would be, no matter if there were a hundred photographers taking pictures trying to make the night perfect. I've even seen women who try to kiss men, and they stick out their hands for a handshake or bob and weave out of the way."

Her voice began to crack from sobbing uncontrollably, and she couldn't finish the words she was about to say.

I pulled her tight to my chest wanting to absorb her pain. The sleeve of my shirt got wet from her tears. I wanted to say something to comfort her but feared if I tried to reason with her, I'd dig a hole so deep, I'd come out in China.

After some minutes of silence, she pushed me away and stood up. She looked up at the moonless sky covered with a thin haze of low clouds. No happy stars twinkled up above. I couldn't even make out the clusters of constellations that Catherine and I had traced with our fingers many nights ago.

"I'm not mad because you two kissed for the whole world to see. It was hearing her say that you had an agreement to be together again even if one of you gets involved with someone."

"It's not like that," I replied. "She's drunk and saying all kinds of lies."

"Lies? I think you're the one lying to me. You're no different than Pierre."

"Look. We had an agreement before she left that if one of us found someone, then we're officially done."

"Did you tell her that when she called you?"

"I was going to but ..."

"But what? You want to have two flavors of ice cream and decide later on which one to toss in the trash?"

"Why are you saying all this nonsense? I've been honest with you since the day we first met."

Catherine shook her head. "It's just that everything is so wrong. Maybe the two of us being together is wrong."

"What do you mean? You are the one I want, and I know you want to be with me too," I replied.

"Seeing you and Meggy tonight reminded me of everything I've been running away from. My old life. My real life. My family. Maybe getting together was some cruel test to see if we're really meant for the people who loved us before we met." She wiped the tears running down her cheek with the back of her hand.

"What we feel for each other is no lie. We both know that," I said.

"When you first told me how you felt about me, I silently walked away from you. Do you know why? I feared that something like this might happen. That the people we loved before might come back. I wanted to stay away from you, but I could not. I feared that a day like today might come. I ignored that and followed my heart. And then this happened. Robert, I think we are not really meant for each other," she said unapologetically.

"Please don't say that. Forget all that karma crap. You never know what could happen at any given time. Forgiveness is what love is all about."

"Then how come it feels like we're prisoners to our past? Pierre wants me back. He's been talking to my parents, and he said he'll stay home if that's what it takes to keep me. I didn't tell you because I didn't want to lose you, but seeing you two up on the stage . . . You look so good together. She's so pretty. You're a perfect pair. And I know how you felt about her. She broke up with you. Had it been the other way around, I wouldn't have been so bothered by it. The feelings of that first true relationship are still strong. She'll always be in your mind even if we're together."

"I'm over her. I told you that when we first discussed our past. If I was still not over her, I would have just walked away from you when we met again that time you were serving tea and said nothing, when you couldn't fit in the car."

"What's the future for us?"

"Love for each other, a life full of adventure, just like we talked about. You and me together until the end of time," I said.

"You're an American and belong here. I'm here temporarily and will be going back to my country soon. We don't even have a concrete plan for what we're going to do after May. I can probably extend my visa for another three months after graduation. That's if it even gets approved. Then what? We'll eventually be torn apart. If not by our past lovers, then by the reality of our situation."

"We can fix this." I reiterated.

"With what? Glue?" She began walking away from me.

"The way we planned it. By sticking together and facing everyone together."

"I think we should stop seeing each other. Soon, many people will get hurt. Not just us. My parents will be disappointed in me, and I don't want to hurt them."

"The two of us should elope."

"Robert, our situation is so difficult. Go back to Meggy while she still wants you. I'll go back to my country and to my old life."

"We can't let what's happening tear us apart," I implored.

"We'll be graduating in six weeks. Most guys would probably treat this as a college fling," Catherine said between sobs.

"You're not just some college fling to me!"

Though her words stung, they had a layer of truth. How could we be together when our worlds were so different? What would happen once the semester was over? As soon as the "Graduation March" played in the background, our relationship would essentially be over.

Maybe she was right. It was better to end everything tonight. Our brief encounter was just a dream. It was pointless to go on seeing each other. She couldn't stay here forever by merely extending her student visa, and I couldn't see myself living more than seven thousand miles away from everything I'd ever known. It would be better to cherish the memories in our hearts. We were both aware that something like this could happen. Our fate was already written in the stars long before our initial kiss. Painful as it may be, perhaps it was the only way to go.

I reached for her hand and pressed it to my chest. I wanted her to feel the vibration of my heart shouting her name. Her hand was cold. I could tell from the resolved expression on her face that we were officially over. We had reached the end of the line, and there wasn't anything I could do to turn things around. Perhaps she was right. Our situation was impossible to manage, and our past weighed heavy on our shoulders. I looked directly at her eyes, reddened by her tears, knowing I would never gaze at them ever again.

I couldn't believe what had happened tonight. One moment, things between us were great like a sandcastle proudly standing on the beach. In a flash, the ocean waves tore it apart.

Catherine firmly pulled her hand from mine and walked away from me, heading back to her dorm.

A lake of tears formed in my eyes. We were supposed to be happily holding hands until the end. Why did it all end so senselessly? I thought of Daphne fleeing from Apollo while she turned into a laurel tree. I could never have her now. In no time, Catherine would be nothing but a memory, just like the laurel leaves on Apollo's head—a reminder that she once loved me but could never be mine.

18

The first week of May finally arrived, bringing the dreaded week of final exams. If thinking about Catherine had brought me down emotionally, the upcoming tests weighed heavily on my mind. I worried about the mountain of textbooks I had to skim and the term papers I had to finish. Just thinking about them put me close to a catatonic state.

As I exited the library, I noticed the students with somber expressions on their faces. No one seemed to be in the mood to party. Everyone was focused on completing their schoolwork and anxious like me to get the semester done and over with.

In two and a half weeks, school would be over for many of us.

I thought of the troubling news that my school counselor left on my answering machine a few days ago. His message had a sense of urgency. He wanted me to stop by the office to discuss my grades. While walking across the campus on my way to the Office of Advising & Evaluations, I tried to push the worries out of my head.

I arrived at the crowded reception area.

"Robert," I said to the undergrad receptionist.

She wrote my name down on her sign-in sheet and instructed me to wait. With the place half empty, I found an open couch, sat down, put on my headphones and listened to a mixtape of rock and roll. The fourth song was about to begin when I saw my counselor, a tall, middle-aged, African-American man with oval glasses walking to the reception desk. Mr. Williams picked up the clipboard and began scanning the names on the list. With his vast experience in academics, he had been instrumental in guiding me throughout my four years in school. I got up and followed him to his office.

He sat behind a large wooden desk with several folders and papers neatly arranged on top.

I sat on the chair and faced him.

"What happened to you this semester?" he asked candidly.

"Nothing in particular that I can think of." I pretended there was nothing out of the ordinary.

"Your history professor reached out to me. You're in danger of failing the class."

The news wasn't a surprise to me. I scored a "D" on one of the major exams. All because I had been so distracted by my breakup with Catherine.

"I've been studying day and night for my next exam."

"You must get at least a C+. You're up the creek and only have about two weeks to prepare."

"It's just, well . . . things haven't been easy lately."

He leaned back in his chair and with a relaxed gesture placed his hands behind his head. "Robert, I'm not just your academic counselor, you know that. I've come to like you since you were a freshman. You can talk to me about anything. You know that, right?"

"I know. The past month has been tough. My girlfriend broke up with me, and I'm taking it hard." I looked down on the floor, ashamed of what I had come to and acutely aware that I might not graduate if I didn't pass the upcoming final exams.

He leaned forward and looked me straight in the eye. "I understand what you're going through. Look, I'm just trying to be objective here. You've already lost her, and if you fail your classes, you'll be in a worse situation. Please concentrate on your studies in the next couple of weeks. Pass your classes. Graduate. After that, you're free to mope all day."

19

Call it unfair, but half of my overall grade depended on my final exam grade. It was a cruel way of evaluation, but it had been the system for years. I sat in my desk chair trying to remember everything that I had been studying the night before. As the history professor and his assistant placed the test papers on the desks, Catherine's image began to crowd my mind. I closed my eyes and tried not to think about her, but as soon as empty space filled my vision, my moments with her played on the back of my eyelids as if they were the silver screen in a dark theatre. We were strolling in a field of wildflowers somewhere in the desert—holding hands without a care in the world.

I asked myself if our appeal for each other was a simple case of an Asian boy, fascinated with the kindness and the unfamiliar accent of a girl from a faraway place. Or was it a European girl attracted to someone whom she deemed interesting? A girl who came thousands of miles to forget the complications in her life ended up meeting me. I didn't realize it then, but the attraction we had for each other was like fireworks lighting the night sky. It had already begun to dissipate even before we had the time to figure out how to keep the flames alive. We were cocooned on borrowed time. Like an experiment in a chemistry lab, our love was meant to stay within academic walls with no practical application in real life.

I pushed the thoughts of her away and concentrated on the test I had to take.

There was nothing worse than being heartbroken while taking a final test.

I sat quietly at my desk and waited for the exam to start. I scanned the room. The students sat with a desk space between them. Everyone was silent and preoccupied, swimming in their own little world. I noticed my reflection in the window. My obsidian hair was disheveled. My eyes looked like the heavy bags that boxers practice on. The instructor wrote the begin time on the blackboard. Noticing the tiny dust mites rising in the air, reflecting the early morning light, I wished I could float with them to a place where there was no more pain or hurt.

Two hours later, the instructor went around the room and collected the test papers. I handed in my answer sheet. Immediately I felt a sense of relief, confident I passed. Hell Week was over, but my heart lingered in purgatory.

MY HEAD THROBBED IN PAIN FROM THE INTENSE EXAM; I WANTED to clear my mind and blow off some steam. The thought of taking my surfboard and heading down to the beach was tugging at me. On my way to the parking structure, I passed by the Scripps Cottage by the green grass. A Hispanic girl with a friendly smile holding the "International Tea Hour" sign stood on a path and waved at me. "Want to join us for tea at social hour? It's relaxing after an exam."

Still early in the day, I decided to stop for a hot cup. While I took a sip, I noticed the tip jar on the table. I pulled out a dollar from my wallet and dropped it in the slot.

The soothing tea began to loosen the muscles on my neck that had been tensed from taking the exam. I glanced at the tree where Catherine and I had sat together for hours. I wished I could run my fingers through her soft, silky hair again. I missed the days when I rested my head on her lap, listening to rock and roll music on my headphones while she read her favorite books. Her hand rested on my chest with the butterfly ring still on her finger.

After finishing my tea, I thanked the students hosting the event. Not feeling like going home just yet, I decided to go for a drive. I got on the freeway heading south. I had just passed the downtown area when the Coronado Bridge sign appeared. Impulsively, I steered the vehicle toward the exit.

Standing on the beach, I could see Hotel Del Coronado's massive, red, cone-shaped roof poking the blue sky. Military jets flew overhead as they circled Naval Air Station North Island. I kicked my sandals off and walked on the soft sand. The edge of the wave touching my feet was refreshing. With the cool wind blowing in my face, the pressure from studying and finishing up my school projects from the last two weeks began to dissipate.

I closed my eyes and began thinking on what I should do next. The low rumbling of the waves crashing on the shore filled my ears. I remembered the things Catherine and I had done while we were together. She was always perplexed at how so much sand ended up in her shoes after we walked on the beach. How we cuddled in bed when she slept over at my apartment. How we stared at each other until falling asleep. She had a habit of rubbing her ankles on my calf, sending ripples of ecstasy up my spine. I remembered her red pedicure sparkling in the early morning light.

I reminisced about waking up on Sunday mornings in my bed with her legs wrapped around mine. I would make her favorite breakfast: French pressed coffee, sliced apples with yogurt, pancakes, and omelets with cheddar cheese and mushrooms.

Her scent lingered on my bed sheet for days long after we made love all night.

Often, we talked about the places we would travel and the things we would do. We were going to build a future together, but it wasn't well-defined. The only way to keep our love going was to seriously commit to it. Maybe she was sending me a message by wearing the butterfly ring every time we were together.

I thought of her last words when she said we weren't meant to be together. Did she actually suggest we couldn't be together because of her immigration status? She was not ready to settle down, but maybe she didn't want to admit it. I remember the yearning expression on her face when she was looking at the diamond ring in the window. I was the key, so she could legally stay here. What woman in her right mind would tell her boyfriend to marry her so she could stay legally? The only way to prevent Catherine from going back to her country and vanishing from my life was for her to become my fiancée. What was the point of waiting anyway? I was a hundred percent sure that I needed her next to me every waking moment. Though I was well aware we were still very young to settle down, life would be meaningless without her. Why prolong the inevitable when being with her was the only thing I wanted in life? Asking her to marry me was what she wanted to hear from me all along. She needed reassurance about how much I loved her.

Then all of a sudden, something clicked in my mind. Of course, we were going somewhere together. We were going to build a future together. It's just that our plans weren't well defined. The only way to keep our love going was to seriously commit to it. Maybe she was sending me a message when we were looking at the diamond ring in the store window. Perhaps she was ready to settle with someone. And that someone was me.

The only way to prevent Catherine from going back to her country and vanishing from my life was to ask her to marry me. She was hiding from me somewhere in the forest and I must find her before she vanishes and turns permanently into a laurel tree.

20

I walked inside a jewelry store with the $300 cash I won from the fundraising. Apart from the two older couples looking at the necklace and rings on display, the place was empty. I scanned the different rings in the glass cases. I had no idea what to pick or if I could even afford one since I've never shopped for a ring, even for myself. There were so many designs to choose from. Some of them cost more than $2,000. Doubting if I was doing the right thing or if I was making a big mistake, I took a step back and inched my way back to the door.

The saleswoman, her hair tied in a bun, which made her look like a prison warden, stopped me before I could escape. "Can I help you find something?"

"I'm looking for an engagement ring, but I don't think I can afford one. They all look so expensive."

She moved a few steps closer, flashed a smile as if she was a trustworthy neighbor who was going to give me cooking advice.

"There's always something for everyone."

"I'm just a college student."

"Let me guess, you're thinking of popping the question to your fiancée?"

"I'm going in that direction."

"How much are you willing to spend?"

I reached into my front pocket and pulled out the folded bills. "It's all I have."

"Follow me. I'm pretty sure I have something within your budget that you'll like."

She pulled out several diamond rings from the glass case and laid them in front of me. She began educating me about the different cuts of stones and types of bands. Each ring had a unique beauty and character. I agonized about what to pick, going back and forth between what I liked and what I could afford.

"This one." I pointed to the one that interested me: a solitaire diamond perched on a band of white gold. "Do you have a student discount?"

"No . . . but it looks like it's within your budget. Let me see what I can do," she said punching numbers on the calculator.

"OK."

The total with tax was a few dollars over $300.

"Since you're paying cash, $300 is fine. Student discount," she said, winking at me.

"Thank you."

Her eyes sparkled brighter than the stone I just picked, looking happy she made the sale.

I pushed the money across the glass counter. She placed the ring in a box and handed it to me. By offering the ring to Catherine, I hoped to wipe away the cloud of doubt hanging over her head. This would prove to her that I did not intend to get back with Meggy and that we were meant to be together. She could get her green card and legally stay in the country without fear of deportation.

I carefully placed the small box in my jacket pocket and

hurried out the door, ready to once and for all get to the heart of our unfinished business.

Our future together.

I STOOD IN FRONT OF CATHERINE'S DOOR, DETERMINED TO KNOCK until my knuckles bled. I started thinking if I saw her, I'd grab the book she's reading and put the ring in-between the pages. When she opened it, I could say, "I finally know how it ends. Look at page 199." The ring would be there.

After several minutes of constant knocking, there was no answer. Curious of what was going inside, I placed my ear on the door but only heard emptiness on the other side.

Lost and not knowing what to do next, I sat on the floor, leaned against the wall and put my head down hoping she would arrive soon. Ten minutes later, I heard footsteps coming from the end of the hallway. When I looked up, expecting Catherine to be coming in my direction, I was disappointed to see that it was the Brazilian girl who lived next door.

"Looking for Catherine? She hasn't been staying here," she informed me.

"How long has she been gone?" I asked, standing up.

"Let me see," she replied, putting fingers below her chin. "About two weeks? She took her things and just left."

"Do you know where she went?"

"Sorry, don't have a clue," she said with sympathy in her voice.

Her news saddened me. I wondered if I'd ever find her again.

"We had a bit of a problem and . . . Has she left you a forwarding address?"

"Yes, but . . ."

"She probably told you not to say anything if you see me?"

"She seemed upset when I saw her packing her things, but

she didn't say that I couldn't pass her address along. Hold on, I'll get it. It's in my room."

I was relieved that I could finally see Catherine. She handed me a piece of paper, feeling ecstatic and imagining that I would be at Catherine's doorstep in less than an hour. I immediately scanned the information. My heart sank when I read it was her Andorra address. It was useless. I wanted to know where she was staying in town.

"I'm sorry, but that's all I have," her next-door neighbor said.

Desperate to find her, I ran across the pedestrian bridge and onto campus. I hoped that I'd find her either at the cafeteria, the library, or in an empty classroom. Walking past a residential hall and fraternity row, I imagined the frat boys partying and already forgetting the semester.

I made my way back to the transit area. Students were getting on and off the buses.

I searched the courtyard at the student center. Students stood idle near the potted plants talking. Still not a trace. I checked the people sitting at the tables and in the study area enjoying the warm San Diego sun, hanging onto a thread of hope that Catherine might be one of them. No luck.

Perhaps by some miracle, she could be walking at the main promenade on her way to the library or the administration building to take care of last-minute business, I headed in that direction. When I arrived, a group of prospective students and their parents were clustered together while the school guide pointed to the important buildings that future students might find useful during their stay at school. Still no Catherine.

I inspected the places where she usually hung out like the cafeteria, hoping she was reading a book. She wasn't there. Not knowing where to go but hoping she might be there, I went inside the music building. I walked past the practice rooms. The sound of a jazz band playing vibrated through the door. There wasn't even a trace of her perfume.

I ran to the places where we talked for hours. I checked each classroom as I passed by, peeking inside with a thin thread of optimism, but saw only rows of empty desks.

On the school cafeteria's back patio, where we once kissed and read poetry, I only saw two people playing chess.

I headed to the small patch of garden in the courtyard near the planetarium. Except for a student lying on the grass with headphones, no one was there. The flowers along the buildings caught my attention. They used to be so vivid and magical, but now monochromatic and lifeless. My search wasn't producing any results.

Not wanting to give up yet, I searched the library. The slanting light from the late afternoon sun peered through the thin-slivered windows, illuminating the rows of books. I raked through the aisles, confident that she would be tucked in a chair, reading. After checking the bottom floor, I was disappointed to see that she wasn't there at all.

I ran up the stairs, passing by the stainless steel discs that were stacked like flying saucers as an art piece in the middle of the staircase. While rounding a corner, I heard two women talking. My heart skipped a beat, when to my astonishment, I heard one of them with Catherine's familiar accent. I reached in my front pocket and felt the jewelry box, readying myself to present it when I see her.

I raced across the room. The same voice that I had fallen in love with was just around the bend. As soon as I was within arm's length, I called out, "Catherine"

The two women turned to me, startled look on their faces with my abruptness. I was disappointed to see that neither one of them was Catherine.

"I'm sorry," I said in an embarrassed voice. "I thought I knew one of you."

They shyly smiled and resumed talking. I quietly walked away with no roadmap on where to find her.

Not wanting to give up, I scoured the hallways of the school's main building. Flyers advertising test preparations for GMAT, CBEST, LSAT, GRE and a semester abroad with pictures of students holding beer steins in some beer hall were pinned on the boards.

I ran straight to the payphone on the side of the building and dialed her number. It rang more than 10 times until I heard the disconnect sound. Anxious to talk to her right away, I dialed Brooke's number; maybe she knew where Catherine was, but it too rang several times, till the answering machine picked up. I slammed the phone back on the cradle, feeling my search was futile.

Lost and not knowing what my next step should be, I stood at the arched window of Hepner Hall, looked down at the sundial's direction and watched the students walking by with faint hope that she would pass by . . . she never did.

THAT NIGHT, I LAY IN BED AND STARED AT THE CEILING WONDERING where I could find Catherine. The prospect was bleak. I turned toward the window. The pastel yellow crescent moon hung alone in the night sky. I pondered if she'd have a view of the moon from where she was. Was she looking at it at this very moment as well?

I whispered to the moon, "Catherine, wherever you are, I want you back."

Somewhere in the far distance, a star winked at me.

Perhaps, it was just my imagination.

21

At least 10 students were waiting just outside my history professor's office when I arrived, chitchatting about their plans after graduation.

I approached a guy I knew from class who stood by the door, "Are the grades up yet?"

He scratched his brown beard, then adjusted his dark-rimmed glasses. "The professor and his assistant are still inside checking our grades."

My heart palpitated as I waited for the door to open, anticipating the results. Five minutes later, the professor's assistant walked out of the room. She taped the sheet of paper with our final grades on the door. Simultaneously, everyone rushed to check his or her grade. The student names were blocked, showing only the letter grades with each individual's last four social security numbers for privacy. I scanned the list. As soon as I saw my number, my heart rate quadrupled—this time because of joy. I scored a "C+" for my overall grade.

I was going to graduate.

"You look like a happy camper," said the bearded guy.

I high-fived him. "I'm over the moon, man!"

"Get your graduation picture taken. Today's the last day," the bearded man said, walking away.

A LONG LINE OF GRADUATING SENIORS FILLED THE HALL WHEN I arrived at the student center. I approached one of the staff members sitting behind the table and gave her my name. She checked my student identification card, crossed my name off her list, then handed me the cap and gown to wear in the photo shoot. While I waited for my turn to get photographed, I remembered Catherine had mentioned that she wanted to get our picture taken together. That was only wishful thinking now. When it was my turn to be photographed, the photographer fixed the tassel hanging on the side of my mortarboard and told me to sit down.

"Take a few deep breaths, then give me that million-dollar smile."

As I balanced my weight on the stool, I thought of the four years I had spent as an undergraduate—the feeling was bittersweet. The whole college experience felt jaded and incomplete, all because Catherine had probably flown back to Andorra without even saying goodbye to me.

I forced a smile, then the flash burst in my face.

WITH THE SEMESTER OFFICIALLY OVER, THE GRADUATING STUDENTS were already moving on and forgetting about college, including me. There was a myriad of activities happening on the campus grounds. After exiting the student center building, I noticed white canopies set up in front of the administration building and a big sign that said Job Fair. Curious, I joined the other students browsing through the booths with incentives and promises of great pay and travel to exotic places. A giant sign from a well-known financial corporation advertised that the company would pay for moving costs and first month's rent, if hired.

A booth hosted by a local television station caught my eye. A tall, slender woman with wavy hair greeted me with a broad smile.

"Ever think of a career in television?" she asked.

"My major is in television and film," I replied, "Of course."

"Good. You came to the right place."

"Are you hiring?"

"That's why we're here," she said. "Are you graduating this year?"

I thought of my grade on the paper taped outside my professor's office. I said proudly, "Yes, of course."

"We're conducting several interviews."

"I don't have much work experience, but I worked as a photographer for the school paper and did some video editing."

"We have plenty of entry-level positions. Fill this out with all your current information and list all the work you've done," she said, handing me a job application.

I wrote everything I could remember from the years I worked for the school paper. I even mentioned winning the charity auction. Satisfied with all the information included, I handed her the completed form. I doubted if I would even get a call.

"I'll forward it to the hiring manager," she said. "Here's my info. Call me after two weeks if you don't hear anything from anyone in the company."

I slipped the recruiter's business card in my backpack. As I was turning to leave, I saw Ryan and Brooke perusing the brochures a couple of booths away.

With high hopes that Brooke might know where Catherine was staying, I strode toward them.

"You OK? I spoke to Catherine a week ago, and she told me about your breakup," Brooke said, stepping closer. "I'm really sorry."

"It's OK. Do you know where she's staying? I really need to talk to her," I asked.

"I don't know. She won't tell me either. She calls me whenever there's something important she needs to tell me. She doesn't want you to know where she's staying."

"She'll be at your wedding, right?"

"Robert, um . . . we have a problem. When I talked to her a week ago, she said she might not come since you're the best man."

"I'm sorry I got you involved in this mess," I said, miserable over how Catherine had already erased me from her world.

"I understand. Things happen," Brooke said.

"I might have ruined your big day," I said, feeling sorry for the chain of events.

Brooke pulled me toward her, gave me a tight hug, then said in a consoling tone, "It's going to be all right, Robert."

"I saw this number on my caller ID when she called about four days ago. She could be anywhere in the county though. I tried calling it, but it goes straight to the answering machine. I think she's screening all her calls and I doubt if she'll talk to you," Brooke said.

I took the piece of paper with the scribbled number and stuffed it in my front pocket.

"You better show up at our wedding, or I'll hunt you down." Ryan followed up with, "Your tuxedo is already paid for."

22

With renewed hope of finding Catherine, I dialed her number. With each ring, my heart skipped a beat in anticipation of her picking up. But after the phone rang five times, the answering machine beeped, then I heard her voice in a plain greeting announcing the phone number and to leave a message. I wanted to say something and make a lengthy declaration of apology and plead to her to call me back. The thought of it sounded pathetic. It would only make me look desperate and would probably ruin any chances I had of getting her back. Dejected, I hung up the phone, crumpled the piece of paper with her number and threw it in the nearby bush.

Walking back to my car, I told myself to forget about her since the chances of us getting back together was highly unlikely. As I looked up at the sky above, the trail end of the cloud floating by began to unveil the sun behind it. There might be a silver lining to my dilemma after all. I began to think ... If one knows a person's full name, usually his or her phone number was listed in the phone book. If I had a phone number, maybe a book cross-referencing a person's address existed. The thought of it excited me. I hurried back to the phone booth where I threw the piece of paper.

I crouched down and felt around the base of the green bush. There were several papers scattered in the vicinity, and it was hard to discern which was mine. It crossed my mind that a snake might be coiled behind the plants and bite my finger, but I didn't care. Then, almost by dumb luck, I found the piece of paper tucked in between the leaves. I plucked it out and headed straight to the library.

I APPROACHED THE LIBRARIAN SITTING BEHIND THE REFERENCE desk, my heart thumping in my chest, scared that there was no such reference book.

"Excuse me, ma'am, is it possible to find a person's address if I only have the phone number? Like a reverse phone book or something?"

She took off her reading glasses and stared at me as if I was a stalker looking for his next victim's address. She said, "Of course."

Her revelation sent a jolt through my spine, reviving my hope of finding Catherine once and for all.

She ambled to the reference section, and I followed her. I watched her flip through the reference pages and combed through the numbers listed sequentially. My pulse pounded at my temples so hard it could knock the books off the shelf.

A few minutes later, she gave me a disappointed look.

"It must be a new number. It's not listed. The reference books were printed a few months ago," she said. "Come back in a month for the newer edition. Maybe it'll be listed by then."

"In a month? She'll be gone in a week," I mumbled to myself.

Her words felt like a deathblow. It was the end of the road for me.

"Thanks for your time," I said, feeling defeated.

I hooked my backpack's strap, lifting it from the floor. As I headed out the door, the librarian stopped me.

"Wait. Usually, the first three numbers belong to a certain area in the city," the librarian added. "Don't know if you're aware of that?"

"You're right. I heard that the phone company does that type of zoning. Do you know where it might be?"

"If I'm not mistaken, the area code and the first three numbers belong to the Mission Beach area. I'm sure of that because my sister has the same first six numbers."

FEELING A LOOMING HEADACHE, ALL I WANTED TO DO WAS TO GO home and finish off a six-pack of beer and sleep 10 hours. I thought about the librarian's comment about the similarity of her sister's and Catherine's first six digits of their phone numbers. I asked myself, what an odd thing she said. From all the places in the county, how on earth did she come up with Mission Beach?

I turned on the car's ignition and as the engine came to life, a light bulb went off in my head. The answer came to me in a torrent. What was I thinking? Mission Beach. Of course, she was in Mission Beach! Where else would she go and hide away from me?

I thought of Mrs. Johnson and her thick head of red hair.

Opening the glove box, I retrieved the map I used when I went there several months ago. Immediately, the circle I had made on the cross street where the house was located popped out at me. My memory vividly recalled its red roof and dark brown exterior and the paddleboard on the balcony. Not wanting to waste any more time, I shoved the gearstick into first and left the campus confident that I would find her.

The big wooden roller coaster welcomed me when I arrived in Mission Beach. I drove straight to the residential area scanning for the right intersection. After passing through several streets, I spotted Mrs. Johnson's house and parked at the curb. With my legs powered by a renewed hope of seeing Catherine, I ran up the stairs and knocked on the door. After a few tense moments, I heard the lock click open.

"Can I help you?"

"Hi, is Catherine in?"

"What's your business with her?"

"I hope you remember me, Mrs. Johnson. I'm Robert. I accompanied her a few months back to pick up her letters."

"Oh. Robert. Yes. She's not here," Mrs. Johnson said.

"I know she doesn't want to talk to me, but it's important that we speak. Please tell her to come out if she's in her bedroom."

"Are you the young man she's been seeing in school?"

"That's me."

Her face contorted into a degree of melancholy. "I'm afraid she's gone. I believe they are flying back tonight."

"Where? Back to Andorra?" I asked, my voice trembling. "Did she say which airport she's flying out from? San Diego or maybe Los Angeles?"

Mrs. Johnson stood still for a moment. She looked as if contemplating whether she should tell me where. As I waited for her long silence, I pictured myself running to the airport and catching Catherine just in time as she entered the gate. I would shout something like "Catherine, please forgive me! I want you in my life! I cannot live without you!" while all the passengers looked at my scandalous cry.

"I really don't know. Her parents picked her up just a few hours ago. She said goodbye to me, but didn't tell where they'd be going." Mrs. Johnson closed the door.

The news pierced my heart like a dagger. With weakened knees, I sat on the steps while I tried to figure out what to do next. Based on what Mrs. Johnson told me, my search for Catherine had finally ended.

I felt a hand on my shoulder. I looked up. Mrs. Johnson stood over me—her image blurry through my tear-filled eyes.

"I heard her cry like that. From what I could tell, she loved you very much."

"I'm sorry, I should be going," I said, looking up with swollen eyes.

"I'm not supposed to tell you this, but she invited me to her graduation celebration in a pub and grill on the boardwalk." She pointed to a direction a few blocks away. "She's there now with her parents. Go after her and tell her how much you want her. I'm sure she'll take you back."

"Thank you, ma'am! This means so much to me."

I ran back to my car.

A RAY OF HOPE FINALLY SHONE THROUGH THE CLOUDY SKIES. I'D BE seeing Catherine in minutes. I was confident that the day would turn out well like it always does in the movies. I rehearsed my entrance in my head. I would shout out her name as soon as I saw her. The doors would burst open, and she would come running into my arms and tell me it was all a misunderstanding. We would lock into a tight embrace in the middle of the restaurant; our lips sealed in a passionate kiss. The patrons would ignore us like two crazy lovers and go around us. Waiters passing by with trays of food would be mindless of the exhilaration happening between us. Music would swell up in a concerto of violins, cellos, and other string instruments. As the camera pans back, we would be standing in the middle of the city, in the middle of the state, then the entire country. Finally, the light blue dot of Earth would be a mere fleck. The moon would be smiling at us until we were part of the rest of the galaxy.

Today would be the day.

Catherine and I would live happily ever after.

Rounding the corner, I saw a street performer in his 20s with a guitar. He was playing the blues and singing about losing his lover to another man on the day he planned to ask her to elope with him. Digging deep into my pocket, I retrieved several coins and threw them into his guitar case.

I raced across the street looking in both directions, careful not to get hit by the passing cars. With my heart drumming in my chest, I assured myself that in a matter of minutes we would be together again, and all this drama would soon be forgotten. I felt confident that after I apologized to her, there would be no reason why she wouldn't want me back.

From the boardwalk, I saw Catherine sitting by a window with a middle-aged couple, looking relaxed. I figured they were her parents. My heart suddenly filled with joy. I was getting closer to my appointed fate. For the first time in a month, I managed to smile freely.

Catherine's back was facing me. I approached the window to tap on it, so I could catch her attention. A group of six waiters gathered around her table. From the way it looked, they were about to sing happy birthday. I found it odd because it wasn't her birthday. I figured that her parents probably asked the waiters to congratulate her for graduating college. Not wanting to interrupt the special occasion, I stood still for a moment. As if on cue, they parted in the middle like the Red Sea. Then a tall, handsome man with light brown hair appeared from behind holding a long-stemmed, red rose. Catherine turned to him with a surprised look on her face.

Instantly, I knew it was Pierre.

My greatest fear was happening before my very eyes. I wanted to break down the glass and steal Catherine away from him. Though she sat only five tables away from me, she might as well be on the other side of the moon.

Immediately, I felt the cruelty of life, how unfair things are, and how senselessly it takes someone away from one person and gives her to another. Nothing around me mattered anymore. The trees with sweet sounding, shuffling leaves and singing birds that only minutes ago were perfect, now sounded dissonant. If only I could reach the cloud above, I'd punch straight through it. The end had finally come. The Hollywood ending I pictured in my mind less than half an hour ago now had an alternate ending. The kind where everyone in the theatre feels robbed.

Catherine accepted the rose. Pierre knelt in front of her, offering a diamond ring. Catherine sat motionless as she stared at him directly. For a second, I was tempted to jump over several tables and intercept the ring from getting to her finger. But even if I could do it in a single bound, Pierre had already lifted her left hand and slipped the ring halfway up her finger.

There was a sickening feeling in my stomach as if caught in the middle of the earth and sky collapsing together. A sharp pain seared through my chest—a vacuum of sorrow sucked the air out of my lungs. I felt an ache in my heart as if a thousand lightning bolts began stabbing me from all directions. I started chanting, "This nightmare is not real. This nightmare is not real. I will soon wake up, and it'll all be gone. All I have to do is to open my eyes."

It was strange how two people can be in the same dimension in the universe yet can be worlds apart.

I wanted to burst through the front door, cause a scene, pull the ring off her finger and shout "No. Don't accept it. I'm the one you love!"

When the reality of the moment finally hit me, I realized she would never be mine. In no time, she would be a married woman. She had accepted the ring. It meant that she didn't want to be with me anymore. I'd lost her for good. The wheels had begun spinning in her life without me. She would be with her old love—her familiar love; somebody she might not be pleased with, but with whom she would be comfortable enough.

I hated myself for becoming involved with her, but also for letting her get away. One silly mistake, and it had all come crashing down. In my attempt to not be rude and accept a hug and a kiss from Meggy, I ended up hurting the one I loved the most.

Droplets of tropical rain began to fall from the gloomy sky. Coin-size liquid formed on the concrete pathways.

A bucket of tears formed in my eyes and began rolling down my cheeks. A searing pain in my chest burned. I stormed away from the restaurant, not seeing clearly, my eyes muddled with the cold mist of rain. The puddle of water on the pavement reflected the contorted images of the yellow, green, and blue paint of the cars parked along the way. They mirrored how things had become in my life—all askew and screwed up.

Catherine and I wouldn't be riding into the sunset together with the orange sun in our faces as I imagined. Instead, it was high noon in a Western town, and I had run out of bullets in the middle of main street, while everyone watched through their partly opened windows with curiosity about who would be the last man standing. I stared straight into the barrel of a gun—powerless to take my woman away from the man who had his finger on the trigger.

From a distance, I heard the faint voice of the bluesman singing, "My baby ain't coming back."

I wanted to run nonstop until I reached the end of the earth.

With trembling hands, I inserted the key in the ignition, shoved the stick in first gear and drove away. As I was driving onto the freeway on-ramp, I smashed my palm on the steering wheel several times in frustration. The trees along the freeway smeared into a patina of an unrecognizable landscape as I gained speed. I had no clue where to go. I just wanted to be far away from Mission Beach.

About half a mile away near Fiesta Island, the rain falling from the charcoal clouds intensified. I just wanted to keep driving until I ran out gas or till the wind stripped my memory clean of the nightmare I just witnessed.

I pushed the car past the speed limit more than the engine could take. The wind blowing through my ears got louder. My world was collapsing, and I felt I couldn't stop the impending doom.

It became hard to see through my windshield as the curtain of rain intensified.

The engine screamed. The car swayed side to side, and I lost control of the steering.

Everything around me blurred into a collage of jumbled images. The road, sky and hills fused into one. I felt rapid clicks beneath my car as the tires rolled over the buttons on the road. The steering wheel buffeted. The tires helplessly tried to cling to the slick road, but only squealed. My car careened off the asphalt road. Everything was happening in slow motion, but speeding up at the same time.

Next thing I knew, the brush along the road was magnifying quickly. I slammed on the brakes and wrestled the steering wheel to pull away from the edge of the road. I overcorrected. The tires screeched. The car spun out of control. Slowly but steadily, I found myself being sucked in a vortex straight into the black hole of uncertainty.

There was a brief moment of silence. I turned the wheel back onto the road once again, but there was no response. A puff of air picked up the car. All of a sudden, I was airborne. Calmness surrounded me. Then it became quiet. The scene at the Western town flashed in my mind. The shoot-out was for real after all. I started to feel as if I'd now die on the desert sand, wet from rain, the woman I love standing over me crying, with my belly full of slugs.

I pumped the brakes several times, but the car wasn't stopping at all. I turned the steering wheel away from side of the road to avoid spinning out of control, but the pull of gravity was not enough to keep the tire's traction hugging the road. I felt my seatbelt's violent tug squeezing the air out of my lungs. All of a sudden, a deafening explosion of cracking metal and breaking glass filled my ears. My head slammed forward onto the steering wheel. A millisecond later, a sharp pain detonated on top of my head. My surroundings became blurry as a spider-like web formed in the center of my vision. Wanting to soothe the pain emanating on my head, I began rubbing it. It was then that I discovered bright red blood covering the palm of my hand. The sight of it horrified me. Then, the nauseous smell of gasoline filled the damp afternoon air. My first thought was in a few seconds, the car would be engulfed in flames, and I'd burn to death. With the car sandwiched between two large tree trunks, it was difficult to push my way out and roll over to the ground for safety. I was trapped in twisted metals. I tried to move my arms and wiggle my legs free, but I couldn't even shift an inch. The steering wheel was pressing hard against my chest.

It became difficult to breathe. I pushed. I pulled. I desperately tried to squeeze my way out of the car, but each tiny movement became a herculean effort. It felt as if a python was wrapped around me and squeezing the blood from my brain.

With each desperate effort, my exhaustion doubled. I made one final attempt to set myself free because I knew that it was just a matter of time before I would be swallowed in flames.

Then, I blacked out.

I DIDN'T KNOW HOW LONG I HAD BEEN UNCONSCIOUS, BUT WHEN I woke up, someone was speaking to me in a loud voice.

"Can you feel this?" the man asked, pushing his fingers in my ribs.

"Ouch!" I nodded yes.

With his dark blue shirt and the stethoscope hanging around his neck, I could tell he was the paramedic. I knew I would live. But because I couldn't feel my thighs, all the way down to my toes, I began to expect the worse. I could also be paralyzed.

"Good. Wiggle your fingers, please."

I twitched my ring finger and my forefinger. When I tried to move my thumb, a searing pain immediately shot along my arm. "Ah, shit!" I yelled.

The paramedic placed a cervical collar around my neck, then lifted me to the gurney. As soon as I was loaded into the ambulance, it became harder to breathe and the pain in my chest magnified. The paramedic placed a mask over my mouth and nose. The gush of oxygen gave me some relief. Grabbing the paramedic by his sleeve, I complained about the intensifying pain in the side of my ribcage. He took my arm and inserted a needle. Minutes later, I heard the droning sound of the siren piercing the mist-covered air as we sped to the hospital.

I never thought it would all come to this. It all began with a series of unexpected encounters and stolen moments to pursue a new-found love. But those thoughts were regrets now. I desperately gasped for more air to fill my lungs with each heaving pain in my chest, from both the physical trauma I suffered from crashing into the tree and from the shattered pieces of my broken heart.

I lost consciousness.

THE BUZZING IN MY HEAD PERPLEXED ME. DISORIENTED, I DIDN'T know what it was—the siren or a fire alarm going off. There is a point between deep sleep and hours of awakening when one's dreams saturates the mind and put the dreamer into a state where he is confused and not even sure if the sounds he is hearing in his mind are real or not. I was somewhere in-between but as time went on, the dream playing in my mind became strange. I was being taken into places where I had already been. The surrounding buildings were painted in pastel colors and furniture in the room were rearranged. Sofas were in the bedroom and the dining table was in the living room.

The staccato hum returned again.

When I opened my eyes, the pearly white ceiling above blinded me. Where was I? When my eyes re-adjusted to the light, I came to my senses a few seconds later. I realized that I was in a hospital room.

After the fifth buzz, I realized it was the phone ringing on the bedside table. I reached for it and answered, "Hello."

"Robert, I'm glad you're awake."

"Ryan?"

"Yes."

"How long have I been here?" I asked.

"Eighteen years," Ryan replied. "You were in a coma. It's now the future, and I came over in my flying car. It makes hospital parking a lot easier."

"You gotta be kidding me?"

"All night. You've been there almost 20 hours."

"How did you know I was here?" I mumbled with a scratchy voice.

"The police found my number in your wallet. They called me, and I came right away but you were sleeping when I arrived. I hung around for an hour yesterday, then left."

"Thank you for looking after me, bro."

"Dude, why were you driving so fast in the rain?"

I turned toward the window, embarrassed to admit the truth. I could see the cars zooming along the freeway.

"It's hard to explain. I was . . ."

"I spoke to the doctor. Looks like you are going to live."

"Any broken bones? I feel like shit," I asked.

"None. He said that your X-rays looked good. You're just banged up. You might even be sent home tomorrow."

"Oh, speaking of broken . . . how's my car?" I asked, hoping it was salvageable.

"It's totaled."

"How totaled?"

"Totally totaled."

The news about the MG saddened me. I had driven it for more than four years without even a scratch. Now, I had no more chrome bumpers to polish or fenders to wax.

"So, why were you driving so fast in the rain? The cars behind you saw you spin out."

"I saw Catherine's ex-boyfriend proposing to her. I didn't know what to do, so I ran away."

"Wow, that's news."

"I just wanted to disappear. That's all."

"You almost disappeared forever," Ryan said. "Stay alive, buddy. You need your strength to walk on graduation day.

Brooke now has no maid of honor. And I need a best man at my wedding. It'd be hard to find a replacement in two weeks."

"If the doctor says I'm good to go, I'll stand next to you," I said, knowing that even if I had no broken bones, my heart was still broken.

"Call me right away as soon as you're ready to be sent home, and I'll pick you up."

23

Wearing a black robe and balancing a mortarboard on my head, I stood in front of the administration building taking the last few breaths as an undergraduate. My parents snapped pictures, as I forced myself to smile. The day that I had been waiting four years to happen had finally arrived. It was Graduation Day.

"Robert," Ryan said, walking up to me with Brooke and their parents.

"You look like a Roman senator," I said.

"Picture time," Brooke said.

"Where's Catherine?" I asked.

"I think she flew back home and will be attending her graduation ceremony at her university," Brooke said.

Ryan's dad snapped more photos.

After taking lots of pictures, we eventually separated. Ryan, Brooke, and I headed to join our fellow graduates, while our parents ambled to the stands.

The bells from the Hardy Memorial Tower chimed, just as they had many times as I rushed to class. It was the top of the hour. This time, I wasn't in a hurry, and it would be the last time

I would hear the bell's church-like sounds. I had looked forward to this day since first stepping on campus, yet now, I didn't feel the stratospheric elation I'd anticipated. The subjects I had studied during my four years were already a distant memory. I tried to sear the images of the campus into my mind—the administration building, the library, and the student center that I frequented. They all had been so much a part of my life during my fun and arduous four-year college life.

As I got closer to Aztec stadium, the sea of graduating students converged toward the entrance. Just as we were about to enter the stadium, the campus police controlling the traffic slowed everyone from entering. Somewhere in my periphery, I caught a whiff of Catherine's perfume. The same one she wore when we went on our first formal date. I turned to my left, then to my right, desperately searching and hopelessly wishing she would be a few feet away from me. I imagined that I'd feel her soft hand as it squeezed mine. When I turn around, I will see her smile, wide as the Pacific Ocean, directed straight at me. But when I realized I was only surrounded by several hundred students wearing the same black gowns and with their mortar boards slightly slipping from their heads, I knew right away that she was already gone from my life.

I sat in my chair and buried myself in the sea of black togas and perfectly shaped, square mortarboards on the stadium field. The "Graduation March" played in the distance. Thousands of parents and family members with big signs and balloons cheered their loved ones who were graduating. It was a perfect day.

The graduating students with top honors were introduced. Some were going straight to graduate school; some would start internships, and the students who completed their ROTC training would go on as commissioned officers.

The commencement speaker stood at the podium. He said

something about graduation, that it wasn't the end but the beginning of a long life of challenges and adventures. About not giving up and to keep pursuing your dreams and doing the right thing even when there are no rewards waiting. His speech was full of inspiring words, but also with lots of clichés. I absorbed each word as if it was the good luck I needed to make it in the real world.

When his speech was done and all the important guests had been thanked for their contributions, I stood in line with the rest of my schoolmates and waited to get on the stage to receive my diploma. I handed the announcer the card with my name. A few minutes later, I heard my name on the public address system. I walked up to the man in a black gown. To my surprise, it was my history professor.

"Congratulations, Robert." He shook my hand and handed me a black folder with the university's name engraved on the front.

"I made it through your class," I said.

"And now I'm history," he said, winking at me.

I stopped in the middle of the stage, switched the tassel dangling from one side of my face to the other side and raised my hands in the air like a prizefighter who had just won a title fight. I was ready to take on new challenges the world had to offer. Unfortunately, without Catherine.

Cheers erupted, and an air horn boomed from the back of the stadium.

24

With the end of June approaching, I needed to vacate my apartment soon. While putting my belongings in different boxes, I thought of what my next move would be. I had asked my parents to keep my things while I took a month off and drove throughout the country to look for a place to move. The memories of the past events were still too raw, and I hoped that living in a different city might take some of the pain away.

I was just about to place my tennis shoes in a box when the phone rang.

"Hello."

"Robert, it's me."

A part of me wanted to slam the handset back on the cradle and end the conversation. I never wanted to speak to Meggy again. That woman had been the cause of my breakup with Catherine, and the agony I went through after that. Since Meggy wasn't aware of the cataclysmic event she caused when she kissed me, and I didn't want to create any more drama, I remained on the line as if nothing had happened. I wanted to tell her to leave me alone.

"Oh... hi, me."

"We didn't have a chance to talk during the after-party at the fundraising event." Meggy sounded upbeat on the phone.

"I had to leave right away," I said. "There was an emergency I had to attend to."

"I'd like to invite you to my graduation party at our house this Saturday. It's just for the immediate friends and family who couldn't make it to New York."

I questioned if seeing her would be a good thing.

"I'm in the middle of packing. Maybe some other time," I said.

"It's only for a few hours. Graduation only happens once."

I took a deep breath and said, "I would feel like an outsider with your family all there."

"What are you saying? My parents know you well and so do my cousins. You're like part of the family."

"I think it might make everyone uncomfortable with me being there. Everyone knows what happened between us. They might think I'm pushing myself on you. I'm like that guy who doesn't get the message."

"I told my parents that I caused our breakup, and I'm just trying to make everything right between us. I'm not expecting more."

Our long absence from each other made us practically strangers. A big city like New York can drastically change a person, and my separation from her definitely changed my outlook on life. If we got back together, would it be any different this time? I didn't know if I could love her again so easily and effortlessly like I did in the past, especially after everything that had happened between us.

I imagined the series of events at her graduation party. We would be looking through a photo album and reminiscing about the past. With a view of the lake in the background, glistening from the falling sun, Meggy would lead me to the backyard where there would be a large table covered with a crisp, white tablecloth holding lots of delicious goodies. There would be at least 40 people at the party. Some will be talking under the brown, wooden gazebo and some will be sipping cocktails and beers by the barbecue island. Meggy would take me to her dad, who had shown me nothing but cordiality in the past.

I'd sit at the large table while the refreshing wind from the lake swirls around us. Meggy and I would pretend nothing ever happened and pick up where we left off. Her family would be warm to me as they had always been. Her Irish clan reminded me a lot of my Filipino family. Everyone would be talking over one another around the table while passing platters and bowls of homemade food. Blissful days would fill my calendar. All I had to do was get a career job, reserve two to three weeks for vacation and to play Meggy's loving husband while maintaining the status quo.

There was a time in my life when being with Meggy and her family was all I ever wanted. But the euphoria of standing on the highest mountain of what seemed to be an everlasting love was a long time ago. Being flat on my back in the lowest recess of the valley of heartbreak when she left me, I doubted if carrying on a past love affair by stoking the fire would bring back the days that I had longed for after she left.

Because Meggy had always been truthful and honest with her feelings toward me, all I could do was to acquiesce to her wishes.

"Can we meet tomorrow before I say, 'Yes'? There are things I want to discuss with you. Late lunch or early dinner?"

"Late lunch would be good," Meggy said eagerly.

"See you then."

I put down the phone, hoping I made the right decision.

I wanted to tell Meggy that I was ready to bridge the day before our break-up. Why not just bury the painful events in the past and go on with our lives? Forgiveness, no matter how grave the sin, is the key ingredient for loving someone. By taking Meggy back, I was not only exonerating her from the sins she committed against me, but also freeing myself from the pain of losing Catherine. And really, in the world of sin—what she did was just a blip in the grand scheme of things. She was confused, so she moved away and thought it was the best thing to do. Her mind failed to consult with her heart on the decision.

Something came to my mind—a presentation I saw about Plato's "The Republic"—on the way images in this world are manipulated in front of our eyes. Sometimes what we see is not exactly what's in front of us. The film started with several prisoners chained to the floor and facing the wall. There was a fire behind them and several men holding cutouts of animals like elephants and lions. The cutouts were casting shadows of the animal's images. All their lives, the prisoners thought that is how the animals looked. But one of the prisoners escaped. He saw what elephants and lions really looked like. They weren't even near how the shadows looked. He hurried back to the cave and told the others what he saw. The other prisoners laughed at him, thinking he was a fool.

It gave me clarity. Getting back together with Meggy won't fix anything.

As I stared down to the floor, I saw nothing but Catherine's face—only her image. Her crystal-like eyes. Her nose that sloped down just precisely. I closed my eyes to shake her out of my mind, but her image became even more vivid. The way she chewed the bagel the first time we were alone together. The outline of her body as she disappeared through the double doors. Remembering all that, I felt love's warmth flowing in my veins.

I still had strong feelings for Catherine. Even this late in the game. The gravity of my situation was so complicated. I would be lying to Meggy for not telling her the truth of my situation. Most of all I would be lying to myself. Regrets will surely come tomorrow.

On my way to the bedroom, the phone rang again. I hoped it was Meggy calling to cancel our plans. After bringing the handset to my ear, I heard the formal sound of a male voice.

"May I speak to Robert, please?"

"This is he. Can I help you?"

"I'm Art Smith, the hiring manager from the TV station. You did well on your initial phone interview the other day," he said.

I was glad that someone at the station expressed an interest in me.

"I'm happy to hear that," I replied with a smile on my face.

"You weren't able to answer some of the technical questions, but it's understandable, I expected that. That comes with experience, but your textbook approach impressed us. Management doesn't expect new hires to know everything, but we look for a candidate's capability to solve problems."

"I'm glad I did OK."

"Can you come down here to the station? Several people want to talk to you."

"When?"

"Ten tomorrow?"

25

I arrived at the station wondering how my second interview would turn out. I flattened my hair with the palm of my hand to look more presentable. Walking across the parking lot, I noticed the satellite dishes pointing toward the sky. In the main lobby, I told the receptionist, a young woman who looked like she had just graduated from college herself, that I had an interview with Mr. Smith. She looked through her appointment book, then instructed me to take a seat.

Not more than 10 minutes had passed when a tall man with dark brown hair, bald at the top appeared.

"Come in, Robert, glad you could make it on short notice. I'm Art Smith," he said warmly. "One of the station managers is going to Japan for a business trip tomorrow, and I'd like him to meet you before he leaves."

I offered my hand, and he received it with a firm grip.

"Nice to meet you, Mr. Smith."

"Please, call me Art. First, I'd like to show you around before you meet the rest of the crew," he said, leading me to the studio.

Mr. Smith led me through the hallway. He pointed to a large tinted window. I peeked in, curious about the action going on.

"And that's where the control booth is located."

The staff inside looked busy as they adjusted controls and watched the monitors with images of the crew in the field. I felt excitement at the thought that I could be sitting in one of those comfortable chairs someday.

"This is the nerve center of our operation," he explained.

I could see the technicians as they monitored the live feeds from reporters and readied to fade in the next commercial for the appropriate time slot.

"This looks exciting," I said as my eyes widened.

"You haven't seen nothing yet. Let me take you to the studio."

We walked down the hallway past several rooms. Mr. Smith opened the door. We stood behind the camera operators with headsets, their cameras pointed at the newscasters in bright lights, sitting behind large desks with the news station's logo on the front.

After the half-hour tour, Mr. Smith invited me into his office. Two station employees sat on the couches, looking relaxed. A tall man wore a gray blazer. The other man, wearing thin eyeglasses, was in blue jeans and a polo shirt. Mr. Smith introduced them as the heads of studio operations. They greeted me with warm smiles as if I was already part of the crew. I sat down, eager for what came next. For the next half hour, the two men asked me more questions about video editing, camera angles, and lighting. Each time I answered correctly, I noticed grins of satisfaction on their faces. With the interview over, Mr. Smith instructed me to step outside and wait. I mulled over what I said in the interview. There was no wrong way to answer them really, just a better approach to solve the immediate challenges. Maybe I should have mentioned this instead of that. It was too late now. What I said was said, and there wasn't anything I could do. To calm myself, I paced back and forth in the empty hallway. Getting hired at the station would be beneficial for me. Though

I would be starting at an apprentice level, it would be the first step in my career path in the field of broadcasting. I looked at the framed headshots of the reporters and important station employees on the wall. All of them started where I stood at the present moment. Maybe my luck was changing. All I wanted was a chance to prove myself, and I would do my best to thrive.

The door opened, and Mr. Smith summoned me inside.

As I walked into the room, the man in the blazer reached out to shake my hand. "We'd like to hire you. Your starting salary will be 30K a year. How does that sound?"

The news thrilled me. I couldn't believe how lucky I was for getting hired at the first company I ever applied to. I could begin my broadcasting career right away.

"Sir, thank you very much for considering me. This means a lot to me," I said, shaking everyone's hand.

"You'll start work in the fall. The broadcast technician will be moving to the news director's staff, and you'll fill his spot. Is that OK with you?" Mr. Smith asked.

"Perfect," I said.

"Good luck and see you the first week of September," he added.

ELATED WITH GETTING HIRED, I WANTED TO TELL RYAN RIGHT away. I ran to a nearby phone booth and punched his numbers on the dial keys.

"Yellow."

"Dude, I did it. The TV station hired me!" I shouted.

"Congrats, man!" Ryan replied enthusiastically. "You're starting when?"

"In the fall."

"Let's celebrate. I'll round up the guys. Wanna meet at the pub down the street?"

"I can't. I'm meeting Meggy later."

"Oh," Ryan replied.

I could sense the surprise in his voice.

"She invited me to her graduation party at her house, but there are a few things I want to discuss with her first. Talk to you later." I hung up the phone.

THE ORANGE SUN HUNG LOW IN THE SKY WHEN I ARRIVED AT Pacific Beach. Tourists were walking along Garnet Avenue checking out the stores, bars, and restaurants of their newly found beach paradise.

Driving toward the beach, I kept thinking about how I would tell Meggy that I needed time to figure things out for myself. Though Catherine was gone, she still occupied my mind throughout the day. I wasn't ready for any commitments. Surely, Meggy had been presenting her best self, putting her best foot forward to impress me. I could tell her efforts to win me back were sincere. She was trying hard to catch up on the time we'd lost. I could go on as if she had never left me; that I hadn't wallowed in pain; that I had never met Catherine; that I had never spent the last month not wanting to wake up and hoping to die instead. A semi-truck speeding down an open highway surely needs time and space to stop. How could I just slam on the brakes, make a sudden U-turn back to Meggy and forget about Catherine? I couldn't run back into Meggy's arms just because she was the convenient girl to be with for the moment—someone to fill the hole in my heart even when I knew deep inside that Catherine was the only one who could do that. Jumping into Meggy's arms, even if I really wanted to, was just a bandage over my bludgeoned heart that would eventually peel off. Whenever I looked into her blue eyes, all I could see was the reflection of our past, and the love we couldn't restore for a future together.

I had to let go. I needed to die before I could be reborn. Like being dropped in the middle of the Arctic Ocean, the sudden chill snapped me out of the lie that getting back together with Meggy would solve my dilemma. Everything was clear. I needed to forget about her and tell her that there was no future for both of us.

I SPOTTED MEGGY STANDING NEXT TO HER RED CAR IN FRONT OF THE restaurant where we agreed to meet. A smile zipped across her face as soon as she spotted me approaching her. She leaned in and gave me a quick hug. Not wanting to be discourteous, I returned her affection and lightly hugged back, pressing her against my chest.

"Have you been waiting long?" I asked.

"No. I just got here."

I want to tell her right then and there what was on my mind to get it over with. But as I was about to ease into my confession, she pointed to the menu board next to her.

"I'm starving. Let's eat before I pass out."

Wanting not to be confrontational, I followed her inside. The place was half empty when we walked in. The waitress told us we could sit at any table. Wanting privacy, I pointed to the table with a red and white-checkered tablecloth tucked in the back of the room.

"The burgers here are amazing."

"What do they have here?" I scanned the menu.

"There's a burger with teriyaki pineapple and another one with melted Swiss cheese and mushrooms."

Sitting across from Meggy, I thought of the perfect time when I would explain that her long absence had killed my deep feelings for her and seeing each other wasn't a good idea, and to forget about me. If I tell her now, things could get awkward while we ate. So, I waited.

"What are your plans for summer?" Meggy asked.

"I need to be out of my apartment soon. I'm packing my things. What about you?"

"There are several firms that I'm considering working for."

Meggy sipped her diet soda, then said, "I have a pair of tickets for a Broadway show. My parents bought them a long time ago, but they can't go. Would you like to go with me?"

"What show?"

"*Les Miserables*. It's playing at the Civic Center."

"The play about the French Revolution?" I asked.

"I'm glad you're familiar with it. You'll like the action part while I'll enjoy the romantic part."

Catherine and I were supposed to see it together. I found it ironic that instead of going with her, I might have to go with Meggy to see it. I was flabbergasted by life's cruel intentions.

I took a sip of my soda. Paused for a moment, then said, "Can't you go with a friend instead? It's just . . ."

"It'll be more fun with you."

"I don't think it's a good idea. It would be better if I don't go," I said, staring straight at her.

"It would be a nice date. Why wouldn't you come?"

Not wanting to tell her the real reason that seeing it with Catherine was the only time I'd see it, I said nothing and let the thought hang in the air.

When we finished our meal, I asked the waiter for the check and handed him a $20 bill and told him to keep the change.

"Can we go for a walk on the pier? I want to tell you something," I asked.

A Whisper to the Moon

THE WOODEN PLANKS CREAKED BENEATH OUR FEET AS WE WALKED on the wooden structure, passing by the cozy looking cottages built along the pier. I imagined the lovers cuddling inside, lost in each other's arms, making each second of their rendezvous count not knowing that it might be the last time they'd make love.

The now burnt orange sun sank deeper behind the wall of water. Meggy and I slowly walked without saying a word. I could sense that she was curious about what I was going to tell her. Several kids ran past the fishermen holding their fishing rods while their parents chased them. There was a time when I thought Meggy and I would have kids of our own, but that was a long time ago before our situation changed. When we reached the end of the pier, Meggy leaned on the railing and watched the surfers in their wetsuits sitting on their boards waiting for the next big wave to come while I listened to the appeasing sound of the waves crashing on the pylons underneath. I wanted to blurt out what was on my mind but couldn't find the courage to do so. Instead, I stared at the imaginary line that separated the flat sea and the dome of the sky.

"Is there something on your mind? You've been quiet the whole time."

I filled my lungs with the salty air and readied myself to deliver the bad news. Using what my heart dictated as a compass, I forced myself to say the most painful words I could ever say to her.

I cleared my throat, then turned to her, "I can't go on seeing you."

Meggy paused for a moment as if trying to process what I had just said. Lines of confusion wrinkled her forehead. Those blue eyes I had fallen in love with, once filled with charm, now pierced me like an arrow.

"What do you mean? I thought things were going great between us." Her voice was shaky.

Her face, filled with a smile at the restaurant, now sagged in disappointment and confusion.

"I met someone when we were apart."

"Are you still together?"

"We broke up before graduation."

"I expected you'd find someone else while we were separated, but that's in the past now, right?" Meggy pleaded with a hint of hopefulness in her voice.

"I'm still not over her. I can't keep pretending things are OK. Sooner or later, I will just fall apart. I need to figure things out by myself for now. I don't want to be with you with one foot still dwelling in the past. I don't think it's fair to go on pretending things are going to be OK between us if I'm constantly thinking of her."

Tears began to pool in her eyes. I didn't take my eyes away from her. I didn't want to be the executioner but rather simply be the bearer of bad news. My words took her by surprise. Her silence aimed at me felt like a thousand thunderclaps in my head. I never wanted to be in this position, but what could I do? I needed to be truthful and needed to say it before it was too late. We had to end our pretend rebound before we incurred severe damages. She looked out at the sea and wiped the tears streaming down her cheeks with the back of her hand. Seagulls floated in the air several feet away as if eavesdropping on our conversation. A few tourists looked in our direction, but I ignored them.

What I had done seemed cruel, but it was the only way to deal with the torment in my heart. I felt as if I had sliced her heart with a thousand daggers. I stood next to her thinking that by standing really close, it would lessen the pain I delivered.

"You don't want me anymore?"

"You're my first love, and you'll always reside in my heart."

"Then why? She's gone. I'm here."

From her intonation, she was trying to put some sense in my head. I understood what she was trying to do. I was in the same situation when she told me we should stop seeing each other and to try to forget about her. I imagined Meggy screaming in her head, "What is wrong with you? A beautiful girl wants to be with you. Are you blind? No, stupid!"

"I need to sort this out on my own. You once said that if we're truly meant for each other, it will still be us together in the end."

I wanted to put my arms around her to silence the echoes of her cries. As soon as she saw me moving closer, she stepped back and looked away. I never wanted to hurt her, but more than anything, I never wanted to hurt both of us in the long run. The sea wind picked up and stung my face as it dried the moisture that had formed in my eyes. It was like I was the worst kind of human being for hurting the woman who once loved me when no one wanted me.

"Just leave me. I want to be alone."

Standing inches from her, I could hear her sobs drowned out by the sound of the crashing waves below. I stared at the side of her face. The same one I kissed more than a thousand times. White like alabaster; smooth like polished marble. I knew deep in my heart that today would be the last time we'd be this close together. I made an about-face and walked away from her, passing by lovers holding hands. The top portion of the sun's circle dipped below the horizon turning the sky into a swath of crimson and the sea purple.

I blended in with the crowd, wanting to fall off the face of the earth.

26

I looked out the window from my cold and empty apartment. The transparent moon hung low in the sky above the rooftops across the parking lot. It was early Saturday morning. Ryan and Brooke's wedding was scheduled for later in the afternoon. The events of the past semester flooded my mind. I thought of college, Catherine, and Meggy. I finally graduated, yet honestly felt like I had accomplished nothing. Everything was meaningless with Catherine gone. How could we have separated when deep in our hearts we truly loved each other?

With the summer months ahead, I hoped the trip I planned would help me forget what happened during the last semester. Perhaps by going all the way to the far reaches of the Earth, everything would unravel into one serendipitous realization that in the end, I would forever be alone and to just live with it.

I picked up my backpack from the floor and strode to the front door. On my way out, I looked back and gazed at my place. So many things had happened here. I imagined Ryan and Brooke sitting at the dining table laughing at my jokes while we ate pizza. Catherine standing in the kitchen making me a peanut butter-banana sandwich, and me thanking her in the Elvis Presley voice I did so poorly.

My apartment was once filled with laughter and loud music, yet now I heard nothing but the echoes of silence through the walls.

I was about to close the door behind me when I heard the phone ring. I stopped for a moment and asked myself if I should I answer it.

The answering machine picked up, I heard Ryan leaving a message. Troubled that something might have happened, I ran back inside and grabbed the handset.

"Hello."

"Hey, buddy. You coming?" Ryan asked.

"Yeah. I'm already on my way out. Is everything OK with you?"

"We have a slight change in the program."

I could sense worry in his voice.

"Then what's the matter? Are you having second thoughts? If you want to skip town, I'll get you out."

"No."

"Is it about Brooke? Did something happen?" I asked.

"She's fine. In fact, she is getting ready, and she'll be at the church soon. No one is running away, and the wedding is not being cancelled."

A brief silence followed. I heard Ryan taking a long deep breath. I wondered what he was about to tell me.

"No. It's about Catherine. She is coming to the wedding. I wanted you to know that. At the very least, I wanted you to be prepared. There's nothing worse than being caught off guard."

Upon hearing what he said, I almost dropped the phone in disbelief. If she was going to the wedding, there might be some unforeseen drama between us. Sure, no one in the audience would know, but I was almost certain the air would be stifling when we finally met.

"Did Catherine tell Brooke that the only way she would be part of the wedding was if I didn't attend?"

"No, it's not that."

"I thought she's back in Andorra?"

"No. She spent a week in San Francisco with her parents and stayed behind. She's here and wanted to fulfill her promise to be Brooke's maid of honor."

"If Catherine and Brooke are not comfortable with my presence, I understand."

"No, it's not about that. I just want to be honest. I don't want you to think that I'm trying to be sneaky. I just found out this morning myself. You'll be OK, right?"

For a second, I thought of the sudden turn of events. If I didn't show up because of Catherine, then I'd be hurting my best friend. He wanted me to be next to him on his special day, and I must oblige to his wishes as a loyal friend. Brooke might think I'd ruin her wedding by creating more drama than necessary. If I had to stand next to Catherine and sacrifice my pride, I would do it, so Ryan and Brooke could have a joyous day.

"Does Catherine know I'll be there?"

"Yes."

"She doesn't mind?" I asked.

"No. She is set on being there. Brooke is only concerned about you."

"What about Pierre?"

"That was the first thing I asked Brooke. He already flew back to Europe."

I twirled my necktie as I thought of the significant turn of events.

"As long as she doesn't have a knife tucked in her bra, then I'll be there."

"Ha, ha . . ." Ryan laughed sarcastically. "If she has one, I'll lend you my nunchucks for an all-out fight."

27

I arrived at the Mission San Diego de Alcala a half hour before the beginning of the ceremony. Some of the guests had already arrived and were standing outside the church posing for pictures. The florists were placing flowers at the ends of the pews and decorating the area near the altar. I stood next to the votive candle stand and soaked in the calmness before the ceremony began. The scent of burning wick and melting candle floated in the still air. The bridal party was arriving shortly, and soon I'd be face to face with Catherine. I wondered if I should confront her and ask why she decided to accept Pierre's proposal and push me aside, without asking if I'd gone back with Meggy.

Though the wedding vows would only take a few minutes, the celebration itself would last all evening. How would Catherine and I endure each other's presence? How would I try to avoid her? Pretend that I was busy with the rest of the groomsmen? Eventually, we would be at arm's length from each other, and what should I do when our eyes meet? Look away? Smile?

Following the terràcotta brick floor, I wandered into the small garden in the church's courtyard. The pink and purple flowers looked cheerful under the yellowing sky. I peeked through the entryway. More cars were arriving. I checked my watch. The wedding was about to begin in 15 minutes.

Sitting on a bench, I took out a piece of stationery and pen from the inner breast pocket of my blazer. Since there was no chance at all for me and Catherine to say our goodbyes in the evening, I began to write my parting letter.

Dear Catherine,

I'm aware that talking to me is the furthest thing from your mind, but this is the only way I can connect with you for the last time, even if I won't ever hear from you again. Firstly, I'm sorry for the pain I caused you. It was never my intention to trick you. It's just that Meggy was so persistent to get back together. I only want to be with you. I met with her to tell her that she and I were through. Afterwards, I looked for you all over the place to tell you that news, so you would understand that my intentions were pure. But when I heard that you had already left and flown home, I gave up looking for you. Then I knew it was really over between us. There's nothing more that I want on this planet than to spend eternity with you. Please know that, if you didn't already.

That day when we met again at the bookstore, I was trying to forget about you. But as fate would have it, you were standing just a few feet from me. I took it as a sign. Fate had brought us together once again.

I am writing this letter partly to apologize for disrupting your last semester, which would have been a quiet and uneventful time for you. I hope that you may find it in your heart to forgive me. The moments we were together, however brief, were the most magical times in my life. The gray skies that hung over me turned into the clearest blue whenever you were near. Those words that I whispered in your ears when we were alone were true.

I will always love you.
Robert

I reentered the church through the side entrance. Ryan stood by the altar with the rest of the groomsmen exchanging small talk as if they were still college buddies comparing football scores.

"There you are," Ryan said.

"Where's the rest?"

"Brooke and her gang will be here any minute now. They're arriving in style in a limo."

"You guys are leaving for the Caribbean tomorrow?"

"We're packed and ready to go," Ryan answered with a grin.

"I've always dreamt of lying in a hammock tied between two coconut trees with a piña colada in my hand."

He placed his arm around my shoulder. "You OK, buddy? I've been worried about you."

"Thanks for calling me earlier," I said. "It's nice not be caught off guard."

"No problem. Just don't cause a scene. You're not going to . . ."

"Go berserk? It depends," I said jokingly. "If she jumps me, I can't promise anything. It's on. So, what made her attend after all?"

"Brooke might have mentioned that you and Meggy got together. I think she figured that you wouldn't do anything if Meggy's with you. She's coming, right?"

"I only saw her just that one day when I told you because I was going to tell her that there wasn't a chance for us to be together again."

"Well, if that's the case . . ." Ryan replied, shrugging his shoulders.

"Can you please give this to Brooke and ask her to pass it on to Catherine?"

Ryan took the letter from me and slipped it into the inside pocket of his tuxedo jacket.

THE WEDDING COORDINATOR, A PETITE HISPANIC WOMAN WITH A friendly smile, announced that Brooke and her bridal party had just arrived and were assembled in the entryway. The groomsmen and I stood up straight like toy soldiers next to Ryan and anxiously waited for the ceremony to begin. Like Ryan, I was curious to see how Brooke would look in her white wedding gown—how pretty she'd be on her special day. But mostly, I was interested to see how lovely Catherine would be in her bridesmaid gown.

While waiting for the procession to begin, I gazed at the sea of guests in their formal attire. The women looked beautiful in their special event dresses, some had fascinator hats; the men were elegant in their pressed suits.

Not so long ago, I thought I would be in the spot where Ryan stood, waiting for Meggy in her white wedding gown as she walked down the aisle to be my bride, and he would be my best man. It was strange how things had turned out in my life. One day, I was daydreaming about how my own wedding would look like as the groom; next day, I was the best man.

From my vantage point, I could see the outline of the bridesmaids' peach-colored gowns forming halos in the bright light streaming from the archway at the church's front entrance. A part of me didn't want to see Catherine anymore, but at the same time, I didn't want to miss everything that was going to happen throughout the day. How would I react when we were in each other's presence? How would she respond when we finally made eye contact? Would she quickly look away or would she give me a look of disappointment?

The string quartet began playing "Jesu, Joy of Man's Desiring" by Bach. One by one, the bridesmaids started walking down the aisle, taking their time as if they had all day, toward the altar.

Radiant in her peach silk gown, Catherine stood at the church entrance holding a bouquet of flowers. She was the last one to walk down the aisle. I wished I could run to this woman and take her into my arms. The wedding coordinator nodded at her to begin. She proceeded with confidence. She balanced the bouquet of flowers in her hands with such grace as if she was the bride herself. Her honey hair with curls cascaded down her shoulders—bouncing with each step. When she reached the altar, she glanced in my direction. Finally, the moment that I had been waiting for with both dread and anticipation arrived.

She wore only light makeup. It enhanced the smile that spread across her lips. I knew well that it wasn't for me but for the guests. Beads of sweat formed on the back of my neck and rolled down my back. My mouth suddenly felt dry.

Finally, the woman I had come to love for a semester stood only a few feet away. My heart began to beat uncontrollably, the same way it did when I met her again and first declared that I wanted her. One, then two, and finally three seconds ticked by, but neither one of us could take our eyes off each other. Catherine still had the power to make my heart skip a beat. Everyone in the church morphed into a blur. Nothing mattered but being in the same place as her.

Suddenly, the flurry of activity of the small world around us ceased to exist. The music faded away. It was just me and Catherine in an empty church. Me in a black tuxedo, and she in a white embroidered wedding gown. I imagined reaching for her hand, and she'd hook her arm around mine and face the priest standing at the altar.

The sound of the string quartet intensified. As if a bolt of lightning streaked across the dark night, we simultaneously looked away, aware of the hurt we caused each other, as if we were Adam and Eve on the day they were expelled from paradise. Suddenly, the naked gaze once filled with passion must now be covered as if we're ashamed of each other's presence in front of everyone living on the planet.

Seeing Catherine up close filled me with gladness but at the same time devastated my soul, knowing she would never be mine. She joined the rest of the bridesmaids standing at the altar.

THE SOUND OF THE ORGAN FILLED THE CHURCH WITH COMMANDING chords. The front doors opened, and a slight breeze blew in carrying a fresh scent of candles burning. Everyone stood up. Cameras flashed from all directions. Brooke, in her strapless, white wedding gown, glided to the altar, taking her time and savoring every second of her special day.

The guests sat down, the old wooden pews creaking under them. The priest signaled for the two of them to come forward, then recited a scripture from the Bible.

In the middle of the ceremony, Ryan and Brooke faced each other. The bridal party and the groomsmen turned in the same direction. My eyes darted to Catherine, stealing a one-millisecond look. I caught her as she snatched a quick peek at me. Should I give her a quick smile or mirror her expressionless face instead? Not wanting to escalate the tension that was about to blow the church doors wide open, I quickly looked away.

I asked myself, how did we end up this way? A few months ago, we were two people in love, now nothing but pain and disappointment filled our hearts. I glanced at her left hand and saw the shiny band around her finger confirming that she's also a bride to be. Unfortunately, I wasn't going to be the groom.

The priest preached about friendship, openness, and forgiveness and about how they were sacred in a lasting marriage. A cloud of sadness came over me realizing that I might never hear that advice on my wedding day because I might never be married. My lungs almost suffocated with those words. I reached for the knot on my tie and loosened it. Anxious for the ceremony to be over, I contemplated skipping the reception. Was Catherine thinking the same? Maybe she wanted to reach across the aisle, give me a tender hug and mend our feelings before we finally parted ways for good; this way, we could go on with our lives in peace. I put my hands together and looked down at the floor. Catherine and I had so much love for each other, but now, neither one of us could find a morsel of forgiveness to set each other free. We had hurt each other beyond repair.

The priest motioned me to come closer. I retrieved Brooke's ring from my vest pocket and handed it to Ryan. Ryan and Brooke faced each other. Catherine bent down to fix Brooke's wedding gown. The priest asked Ryan if he would take Brooke as his wife. Ryan said, "I do," smiled and slid the ring on his new bride's finger.

When it was Brooke's turn to say her vows, Catherine approached her to give the wedding ring. The ring was attached to a ribbon on Catherine's wrist. One pull from the end of the bow to get it off should be an easy task. Catherine was struggling as she tried to free the ring from her wrist. Ryan turned to me and pointed in her direction. I went around the back of the priest to check why the ring wouldn't come off. Standing inches away from Catherine, I pointed to her hand. Nervous laughs erupted from the guests sitting in the front pews due to the minor snafu. Catherine half smiled with embarrassment. She reluctantly offered her hand to me. Tenderly, I pulled the ribbon apart with my fingers, but it was ineffective. I tried to figure out what was wrong with the knot and realized that the ribbon was tied together so tightly that the only way to release the ring was to use a pair of scissors, but nothing sharp like that was around. Wanting to end the dilemma and end stealing attention from Ryan and Brooke's big day, I put my mouth over her wrist and worked my teeth to loosen the knot. This time, the audience erupted in laughter. Moments passed until the knot came loose, and the ring fell into my hand. I held it high for everyone to see. Applause and cheers erupted.

28

The guests' clapping and cheering inside the reception hall was thunderous. I waited outside with the rest of the entourage as the wedding host introduced us one by one. Catherine and I quietly stood next to each other as if we were two strangers waiting at the bus station avoiding eye contact. By keeping some distance from each other, we could avoid any potential disaster. Though we had been civil to each other up to this point, I could feel the tension between us getting tighter and tighter with each passing second. I just wanted the night to end, go home, and never see her ever again.

I didn't know who to blame. Me, for not avoiding Meggy's kiss and causing her grief, or Catherine, for not understanding that it wasn't really my fault and quickly accepting Pierre's proposal, disregarding me in the process. We were both inside our cocoon of pain and pride. Our issues would never be mended; even a civilized goodbye seemed unlikely.

The doors opened, and the loud music blasted through.

"And here's to Albert and Suzy," the host announced through the public address system.

The groomsman made a dance move pretending to lift the

roof above his head. The bridesmaid swung her hips side to side as they made a grand entrance into the hall. The rest of the entourage followed by either skipping like happy couples or doing funny robot walks showing the guests they were having a good time.

"And now, ladies and gentlemen," the host shouted, "Please . . . a big round of applause. The best man and maid of honor, let's hear it for . . . Robert and Catherine."

The large double doors swung open. The bright lights blinded me. I thought of reaching for Catherine's hand as we walked in to show everyone that nothing was out of the ordinary and that we were just taking part in the evening's fun. But at the last second, I distanced myself from her. There was no point in pretending that everything was OK, because it was not. From the look on her face, she seemed relieved when I stepped a foot away from her.

Cameras flashed in our faces—bright like a hundred suns in the universe. The deafening claps and whistles from the crowd filled my ears. So that our entrance wouldn't look stiff, I made a silly dance move and made circles with my hand in the air, smiled and pretended to be in unison with everyone's genuine joy of the night.

Catherine, not wanting to be the Grinch of the party, immediately joined the fun. Sidestepping and clapping her hands, she danced her way onto the central floor.

The whole world was probably thinking that we were just an ordinary couple having fun; instead, we were two people dying for the night to be over. For a brief second, I wanted to keep going until reaching the backdoor exit and never return.

To my right stood a sculpture of Cupid. He was looking up, stretching a bow and aiming to shoot. His stance seemed to mock me. The adoration arrow was pointed at me and the disdain arrow to Catherine. He played a matchmaker in the past and brought us together. Then, when he thought we had enough fun together, he broke us up. I wondered if it was just a game to him, and the roguish god was just toying with our lives.

The lights dimmed. Ryan and Brooke entered the reception hall, then all the lights in the room simultaneously came on. They paraded straight to the dance floor for their first dance as a married couple. A misty white fog blanketed the floor. It looked like they were walking on clouds. Bubbles blew from the corner turning the hall into a dreamlike banquet in a faraway castle.

As the music played, Catherine stood a few feet from me. I wanted to pull her into my arms and try to put some sense into her head that I was the one who could make her happy. She could still run away from Pierre. But it was too late for any quixotic gestures because, in a few hours, the last chapter of my life with her, both pleasant and painful, would finally come to an end.

She would fly back to Andorra in the next couple of days, and soon she'd be a postscript in my life.

MIDWAY THROUGH THE RECEPTION, THE WEDDING HOST announced that it was time for the maid of honor and best man speeches. Catherine stood up and took the microphone from the DJ. She faced Brooke. The chatter in the banquet room eased. I could see her eyes glistening with tears. As she began to speak, her voice began to splinter.

"I wouldn't be here in America if not for Brooke. She is the only reason I came here while I finished the last semester of college. I've known her since I was a teenager when she came to Europe with her family for a summer vacation.

"It was one ordinary July afternoon when their car pulled into my grandma's bed and breakfast in France. I was staying there for the summer. They mistakenly thought it was the place they'd reserved. The one they were looking for was a half hour away. It was getting dark, and her dad expressed concerns about getting lost. Luckily, rooms were available that night. My grandma was elated to meet Americans, so she offered them a place. Next thing I knew, we were having tea. Later that night, we shared dinner. We talked late into the night. The moment I met Brooke, I felt an instant connection. She slept in my room. We talked all night about everything and anything that crossed our minds, about school in America, about life in America, about boys in America. Around one in the morning, we got hungry. We went down to the kitchen to find something to eat. Brooke made something special for me from flour, sugar, and fresh apples. She baked me an apple pie. From a single slice of the sweet apples and pinch of cinnamon, I tasted America for the first time. I knew then that one day I would come here, meet and love the people that I had known only through books, music, and movies.

"When she got back to the States, we wrote regularly. We shared many secrets. We confided to each other about our hopes and fears.

"Not only she is my best friend, but I also consider her my dearest sister.

To my sister across the pond and to the best friend ever."

Catherine raised her glass at Brooke. Tears began to form in the corners of her eyes. She sipped her champagne then turned to Brooke, and they hugged.

"And now for the best man's speech," the wedding host announced.

I stood up, my heart banging in my chest. As she handed me the microphone, our eyes momentarily met. This time a gesture of congeniality came between us. Her lips parted, revealing a smile. I returned her heart-warming gesture with a bigger smile and nodded my head with approval. The chill of our silent treatment slightly thawed. I could tell she was also exhausted by our clandestine fight that had been going on all night. Since this would be our last time together, I wanted her to feel that I was OK and had accepted our fate.

I wanted a truce.

I gently took the microphone from her hand, placed it near my lips, and said, "Thank you, Catherine. Next time you crave apple pie late at night, you can just buy one at a 24-hour grocery store near you."

I winked at her, then faced the crowd. She rolled her eyes. Everyone laughed.

As the laughter died down, I became serious.

"I would like to propose a toast to Ryan, the man who can't even make toast without burning it. But seriously . . . he's a great person, and I've known him since my freshman year in college.

"He is not only a wonderful friend to me but at times also a mentor. He has always been by my side, through rain, sleet, or snow. Wow! He would make a great letter carrier.

"When Ryan told me that he was going to ask Brooke to marry him, my heart sank. Not because he picked her, but because I realized that my days of showing up at his apartment unannounced with a six-pack of beer or watching action movies till the wee hours of the morning would be limited. With that thought, my sadness turned to gladness. I now know firsthand that true love only comes once in a lifetime. The opportunity to love and be loved, once missed, disappears with the wind faster than we can raise our hand to grab it back into our heart. I am delighted that he found love with the woman who is now sitting next to him. If my unintentional gift was introducing him to Brooke on an ordinary Friday night at a bonfire on the beach, then I have indeed given him the best gift ever.

"Let's raise our glasses for a toast. To my best friend, to your grandson, son, brother, cousin, friend . . . whatever Ryan is to you . . . Hear, hear! To Ryan and Brooke's new life!"

I raised a champagne glass and took a small sip. Everyone in the audience clapped. Ryan stood up, and we hugged. Immediately, the crowd began tapping their glasses with silverware. As the pinging sounds filled the banquet hall, Ryan kissed Brooke.

With the speeches over and the dinner service ending, the lights dimmed, and the DJ turned up the music. The guests rushed to the dance floor. I had fulfilled my promise to Ryan and Brooke to be part of their wedding, but the time had come to put the night behind me. I stood up and quietly walked away from the reception hall—the music fading behind me along with all the memories of everything that had happened in college.

By the wishing well, my shoelace came undone. I knelt to tie it. As I was getting up, I saw a pair of feet with perfectly pedicured toenails on the ground inches from me. I looked up. Catherine stood in front of me holding the letter I gave Brooke to pass on to her asking for forgiveness.

"I just read the letter you wrote," Catherine said.

"You can toss it in the trash," I said, loosening my collar.

"What are you saying, Robert . . . don't the words you wrote mean anything?" Catherine asked. She was startled by my comment.

"I saw everything."

"You saw what?" she asked.

"I went to find you one afternoon. I went to the place where you were staying in Mission Beach. Mrs. Johnson told me you were at the restaurant celebrating your graduation with your parents. I ran to you right away. When I got there, I was shocked to see Pierre putting the diamond ring on your finger. I was outside just several yards away. I immediately ran away because I couldn't bear the pain," I said.

"You're wrong, Robert."

"Wrong about what? I'm not blind."

"You're the one who'd gone back with Meggy."

"What gave you that idea?"

"I came looking for you but when Ryan told me that you were with Meggy, I knew it was over between us."

"That's not true. I tried to forget about you, but my heart kept screaming your name, and my body wailed for your touch. Did you know how bad I felt telling her that I didn't want to be with her even though you were already out of my life? Yes, I'd prefer living in a world without you rather than be with someone I know who will never compare to you. I couldn't live without you. You're the one I want. But it's too late now. You're a woman already engaged. If I can't be with you, then I don't want anyone else. I asked Meggy to meet me in Pacific Beach to tell her that I already found someone new and to stop hoping that we were ever getting back together."

"You're not with her anymore?" Her cheeks became lively, and her eyebrows perked up.

"No," I said, taking a step back.

"I returned the ring immediately and told Pierre I couldn't marry him because I was already in love with someone else. You should have stayed a bit longer, so you could have seen how things went down that day. Do you know how hard it was for me to do that? When I finally had the courage to call you, I immediately called Brooke to ask Ryan, so we could meet on neutral ground to discuss our situation, but she told me that you and Meggy got back together. I was devastated. I felt so betrayed that you were able to forget about me so quickly."

"If you're not back together with Pierre, then what's that on your finger?"

Catherine raised her hand to me and slowly twisted the ring. I was dumbfounded to see the butterfly ring I gave her. The one I won at the carnival game.

"It's your ring," her voice cracking. "I never took it off."

Like trickles of water that form into a stream and connect to a river, regardless of how aimlessly the route meanders through a jungle, it eventually empties into the sea. Catherine and I were still going to be together after all. The weight of the world was lifted off my chest. I felt a sudden lightness in my heart. With that small gesture, I knew that she still loved me.

"Would that someone you love be me?" A smile beaming across my face.

"Of course, it's you, silly," Catherine answered, tears flowing down her cheeks.

I hooked my arms around her back and pulled her closer. We stared into each other's eyes and let our skin fuse together. I held her tight against my chest. Being in each other's arms put me into a euphoric state. She put her hands behind my neck and held me a bit longer as if I was going to disappear from her sight. I closed my eyes while we kissed and breathed in the magic of the moment.

When we pulled away from each other, I vowed to Catherine, "Please don't ever leave my side. I want you to be the first person I see when I wake up in the morning and the last one I kiss before I go to sleep at night."

"I'm all yours, my love," she replied.

I reached down into my front pocket. The tips of my fingers bumped the small box with the diamond ring.

"Now about your status. We need to do something, so you'll be able to stay here longer without getting deported."

"My student visa was extended for three more years. I was

accepted for the master's program at UCSD," Catherine said, happiness quickly filling her voice.

"I was hired at the local TV station, and I'm starting this fall. We could..."

"Live together, you mean?"

"Not just that. You can stay here in America for the rest of your life," I replied. "You don't have to worry how to keep extending your student visa to be with me. Unless you want to get a doctorate degree."

"How?"

"I think there's a thing called a fiancée visa."

"Are you asking me what I think you are...?"

I retrieved the ring box. On one knee, I knelt in front of her like a prince from a faraway land. I took her left hand, gently pulled the butterfly ring off her finger, opened the velvet box, and revealed the diamond ring.

"Catherine, I know that getting married may be something you're not ready for. But marry me and make me the happiest man on Earth. I promise my undying love and to make each day with me full of color."

She stroked my head and said, "Yes. I would be delighted to give you my heart for the rest of my life and to be called your wife."

She offered me her left hand, and I slipped the ring on her finger. She spread her arms, then hugged me tight. We kissed once again—giggling like two teenagers making out in the back seat of a car.

I jokingly said, "Let's see the priest. Maybe we can get it done now."

She pinched me and said, "It's Brooke and Ryan's special day. We don't need to ruin it."

A whistling sound streaming up into the dark sky interrupted us. A few seconds later, an explosion tore through the still night air. We looked up to see the flowery patterns of fresh fireworks blossoming in the night sky. A starburst of multicolor of ruby, purple, and bright amber with a hundred fingers; the man-made stars were being born right in front of us.

Our love wasn't dissipating from the initial burst after all but being born and strengthening every second.

We stood motionless while soaking in the magic happening before our eyes.

The doors from the reception hall swung open and loud Latin music blasted through. Brooke and Ryan were leading a conga line while the rest of the guests flooded the courtyard.

"Stop making out in the dark and get over here," Ryan shouted.

I took Catherine's hand and led her to the front of the line. Ryan handed me a pair of maracas. Catherine wrapped her arms around my waist. I led the group around the courtyard not knowing where to go—going around the tables and posts. Just as the line circled back to the dance hall, I caught a glimpse of the bright yellow moon hovering above the roof.

"Thank you for telling Catherine in her dreams that I love her."

"What did you say?" Catherine asked.

I looked back to her and said, "Nothing. It was just a whisper to the moon."

ABOUT THE AUTHOR

Dennis Macaraeg graduated from San Diego State University. He is the author of two previous novels. *Somewhere in the Shallow Sea* and *Somewhere in San Diego*. When he is not writing, he is daydreaming, reading in a noisy café or taking photographs. He currently lives on the West Coast.

Dennismacaraeg.com
Facebook: Dennismacaraegauthor
Twitter: Dennismac2015
Instagram: Denniswriter

Made in the USA
Coppell, TX
24 September 2021